MAN PASS MAN

and other stories

Ndeley Mokoso

Longman

To the Memory of my late parents,
Mokoso mo Ngomba
and Mammy ma Ndeley
both of Bonjongo

Longman Group UK Limited,
Longman House, Burnt Mill, Harlow,
Essex CM20 2JE, England
and Associated Companies throughout the world

First published 1987

Set in 10/11 Baskerville (Linotron)
Produced by Longman Group (FE) Ltd
Printed in Hong Kong

ISBN 0 582 01681 9

Contents

While the settings are as true to life as possible, the characters in this book bear no relation to any persons, living or dead, nor do the events and situations to anything that has taken place.

Ndeley Mokoso

The Inauguration

The long awaited day had come – 'The Big Day' – which was to mark the official opening of Cameroon's first oil refinery. The opening was by the President of the Republic, Ahmadou Ahidjo, at Cape Limbola in Victoria, Fako Division. The date was 16th May 1981. The opening was the fulfilment of a dream, the oil money had at last come to stay!

Victoria, hitherto nicknamed 'Ghost Town', suddenly assumed the most prestigious titles. Some called it 'Oil City' others just 'OPEC' or 'OPEC City'. The village head of Limbola, about one hundred metres from the barb-wire fence enclosing the refinery, became known as the 'Shah' of Limbola.

Elaborate preparations had been going on. A high-powered delegation from the Presidency, comprising officials of the Ministries of Armed Forces, National Security and Protocol, had made an on-the-spot inspection and assessment of the various stages of the inauguration ceremony and programme during meetings with high government officials in Fako Division and senior management staff of the refinery.

Within the refinery organisation itself various committees had been set up with responsibility for various aspects of the arrangements like entertainment, accommodation, transport, inaugural ball, reception, etc. It had taken exactly ten days for a road construction company to reconstruct and resurface the ten-kilometre road from Victoria to Cape Limbola, working sometimes in the nights with flood lighting.

A special presidential stand had been erected to accommodate about six hundred VIPs. These included members of Government, high-ranking government officials, representatives of foreign organisations which had been involved in the refinery project, representatives of oil refineries in some neighbouring African countries and local dignitaries.

The route had been decorated in the traditional style – white painted stakes and palm fronds. School children had lined the route. Party militants in their red, green and yellow uniforms had assembled. Traditional dance groups had also

1

gathered. Singing and the throb of drums filled the air.

It had rained heavily the previous night and there had been fears that it would continue to rain in the morning. It did not. The local chiefs had kept their pledge. 'It will not rain during the ceremony. We shall hold the rain,' the paramount chief had confirmed and added, 'The gods of Fako will not let it rain.' And it did not rain! There were no rain clouds around Mount Etinde, just overlooking the refinery. The sea was unusually calm. Bright streaks of sunlight appeared in the sky above Bimbia. All these were good omens. Except for an occasional gust of wind which brought down two banners and time and again rolled-over the red-carpet which had to be held down and kept into position by four attendants, the scene was set for the historic occasion.

The Cape Limbola Refinery Project had become a reality – a project next to the hearts of the peoples of the former State of West Cameroon. It had raised their hopes – hopes hitherto dampened by the decline in business and port activities in Victoria. The opening of the Douala–Victoria road, popularly known as 'The Reunification Road', had also contributed towards the decline. Business was at its lowest ebb.

Then there was the swindling era of the racketeers. The firm clampdown by the state's 'watchdogs'. The exodus of businessmen – Victoria had become too hot for these frauds. Some of them just disappeared while others took refuge in nearby Douala. The signboards also disappeared. Some were just abandoned and the stores remained permanently closed. Once in a while a distant buyer called to look for his 'customer' and was told politely 'He don go country'. And when he returned months later he was told that his customer had not returned because he was supervising the construction of his house in his home town.

There were the earlier rumours that the project would be shelved. That Douala had been the final choice. There were doubts that the project would ever materialise in spite of repeated assurances by Government. The local newspapers headed a crusade and published news stories, editorials and articles. Section, subsection and branch conferences of the National Party echoed resolutions urging the Government to

2

implement its promise to site the refinery in Victoria. Decree No 73/135 of 24th March 1973, creating the National Refinery Company Limited (SONARA) with the objective of constructing and operating a crude oil refinery in Victoria settled it. There were resolutions of confidence, support and dedication to Government institutions and National Unity.

Work on the refinery began without any announcement. What struck the population in Victoria one morning in September 1978, was the arrival of a long convoy of lorries and trailers transporting construction equipment and containers. This arsenal included bulldozers, graders, excavators, truckcranes, loading shovels, crawler cranes, compressors, generators and forklift trucks. The convoy, for some unknown reason, halted on arrival at the Half Mile Junction. News soon spread of the mysterious appearance in Victoria of a lot of equipment. A large crowd gathered within minutes, examining the arsenal from a safe distance. Then it finally took-off for Cape Limbola, led by a red-painted jeep with a revolving red warning light and sounding its siren all the way.

A few days later, the bulldozers went to work on the site, pulling down everything in their wake including palm trees – much to the shock and disappointment of about one hundred wine-tappers who had gathered to arrange the negotiation for their purchase. They held a meeting on the spot and arranged for a delegation to meet the authorities.

The delegation was received. They said it was a waste. The authorities could gain some revenue from the sale of the palm-trees. They were prepared to pay 500 frs. per tree. The meeting was brief. Work on the refinery project could not be held up because people wanted to drink palm-wine. The voice of authority was firm. Disappointed, the wine-tappers decided to take action. During the night hired engine-saws went to work. Twenty tappers invaded the site and cut down, without any authority, about two hundred palm trees. Law enforcement officers were called in to stop them. The situation was arrested. They never came back. One of them explained later, 'When the elephant dies, everyone must eat.' They, too, had a right to take their fair share of the National Cake.

The bulldozers tore down the terrain with a viciousness and brutality that left the onlooker with a sense of helplessness, awe and admiration for the strides man has taken in defying and contending with nature. The rugged and uneven landscape was being transformed into a building site. Temporary offices and prefabricated bunkers sprang up as if from nowhere. Access roads were laid out and modern conveniences installed.

Then the housing boom followed. About five hundred expatriates comprising engineers, surveyors and other technicians were expected initially with another lot to follow. The search for suitable accommodation began. Landlords raised their rents. Houses which originally fetched 80.000 francs a month rose to 150.000 francs. They continued to rise to a ceiling of 250.000 francs. Tenants who were not prepared to pay were given notices to quit. It posed a problem for the individuals but the companies had no choice and they paid.

Then, too, there was the influx of people in search of employment. The local offices of the department of labour were jammed everyday by job-seekers. There was also the invasion by prostitutes from far and near to share in the oil money which had come to Victoria. The men with money were easily identified. They wore safety helmets and always carried a yellow rain-coat and one heard a lot of claims by these people. 'I de work for Oil de Final, I get plenty money.' They took bribes from their less fortunate brothers claiming that they would influence their employment with SONARA. Thousands of letters arrived by post addressed to individuals who claimed they worked for SONARA.

There was an interesting incident involving a driver who checked his fat pay packet in a pub. He took all the money from his wallet and started counting. The others looked on quite astonished – he counted one hundred and fifty thousand francs. He looked round proudly and asked the whole lot of them to take a drink on him. It was drinks galore for all. In the end his wallet disappeared. He did not seem particularly disturbed. He looked round the room and said he would make another hundred thousand francs the following week.

4

It was impossible to shop when they were around. They did not bid like everyone else. Whether at the Down Beach Fish Market or New Town Market, they just paid and the traders and market women loved it!

The night-clubs were full and overflowing everyday. The dance floors were jammed to capacity. The hum of voices drowned by the din of blaring loudspeakers and the air stale and choking with cigarette smoke and sweat from cheap make-up. There were the never-ending brawls among the men when the girl had to choose who to go home with. Church Street – the hub of night-life in Victoria – became famous. At one o'clock in the morning you still found the hangers-on still drinking. This was Victoria – a sudden change from ghost town to a prosperous oil city!

The Construction Site took its toll of human lives. There were fatal cases of workers falling from heights, losing a limb or finger, knocked down by falling objects or moving equipment. This is normal in construction sites all over. But the local population soon found a reason. It was that the local 'gods' were angry. No traditional rites had been performed before construction work started. The gods had to be appeased by some form of libation.

Mr. Lafayet, the resident site engineer, had heard of this local gossip. He did not dismiss it as a bit of superstitious blackmail. He promptly dug into his miscellaneous expenses vote. After the payment and performance of the traditional rites of the people the 'gods' were appeased and fatal accidents were a rare occurrence.

All that seemed to have been forgotten. Two years and nine months it had taken to construct this colossal and most impressive complex. It covered fifty-four hectares containing thirty storage tanks, chimneys, towers, miles and miles of criss-crossing pipe-lines, power, production and transforming units, offices, workshops and port installations. It was hard work for the planners and the executors all along the line from the Project Director to the labourer, including the gate-man whose job was merely to open and close the gate at the check point. They all had every right to be proud of the great achievement. It was an example of what international

5

co-operation, expertise and know-how could bring to developing countries.

And now everything was ready for the formal opening. This was indeed the 'take-off'. Cameroon had joined the 'Oil Club.'

The taxis started in the direction of the refinery as early as 7 a.m. transporting passengers from the Batoke Park. It was good business for them. Later the government vehicles and private individual invitees. They had to get there before the route was closed in anticipation of the Government convoy. At 9.30 a.m. the Government convoy rumbled past – the black Mercedes limousines, Peugeot 504's, Datsuns, Corollas and so on. The crowds cheered and waved each time a Mercedes car went by.

At 9.45 a.m. the refinery parking lots and the surrounding high-ground prepared specially for spectators, were crowded to capacity. The radio commentator described the scene before him as a 'sea of heads'. There was a lot of jostling but it was an unusually orderly crowd.

It was an unusually bright and warm morning. Thanks to the chiefs and the rain maker. A pregnant woman and a school girl fainted. There was no stampede. The Red Cross officials in attendance brought their stretchers and the 'casualties' were taken care off at the nearby medical centre.

'Don't forget to carry along that twenty-litre jug with you to the Refinery,' Ndumbe told his wife. 'And make sure you fill it when you get there,' he added. 'I have emptied my petrol tank. I have enough just to get me there. I wish I had a large truck.' His wife protested. 'How can I march with the rest of the women carrying a twenty-litre jug?' 'The other women will also be carrying jugs. Don't you see? We can't miss this opportunity!'

Ndumbe had told his wife the previous night of the elaborate peparations for the official opening of the refinery. All the people in Victoria had been invited specially for a big treat. Fifty cows had been slaughtered and food prepared for everyone to eat. Some of the tanks had been filled with wine and beer for the occasion. Everyone attending the ceremony in a car would have it filled with *free* petrol. The big elephant had died and every Cameroonian had to take his share of the

meat. His wife, Ngowo, had looked at him in sheer astonish-
ment and disbelief and it was clear to Ndumbe that she
accepted his story with some reservation.

At 10 a.m., the presidential helicopter hovered above the
refinery. It flew westwards, then towards the sea, made a U-
turn and descended slowly towards the 'heliport'. The
engines gave out a deafening screech as the helicopter glided
and finally landed, its twirling blades producing violent gusts
of wind and clouds of brown dust. The waiting and expectant
crowd immediately around the heliport either turned their
backs or covered their noses with handkerchiefs.

The door swung open. Then the President emerged. He
raised his hand smiling broadly as a few officials moved to the
tarmac to receive him. The crowd yelled, waved and cheered.
The drums throbbed. The WCNU women took-up their song
— 'Dimabola oba masoma na edube'. The crowd joined. It
reminded me of a football match I witnessed at the famous
Wembley Stadium in England in 1969. The match was France
against England. The score was five goals to nil against
France. The English fans, well-known for their fanaticism,
had started singing 'John Brown's Body', at the dying minutes
of the game. Wembley Stadium with a capacity of about one
hundred thousand spectators erupted as the crowd joined in
the singing, one section of the crowd starting some seconds
after the other and later sections completing the 'Glory, Glory
Alleluya' chorus long after the first. This is exactly what
happened as the refinery crowd sang 'Dimabola oba masoma na
edube' lustily and with great zest.

The Head of State walked down towards the grandstand
flanked by the presidential retinue. He inspected a guard
of honour mounted by members of the Armed Forces. After
the inspection, two little girls in identical immaculate white
maxi-lace dresses complete with gloves, picked their steps
slowly towards the red carpet and curtsied. 'Welcome to
SONARA, your excellency, President of the Republic. Bien venue à
la SONARA, son excellence, Président de la République,' they
repeated one after the other. Then they handed over the
giant bouquet of white and pink flowers. They both turned
their cheeks for the anticipated presidential kiss. The

7

President smiled, bent down and kissed them.

Then followed the decoration of a number of personalities, two addresses by the President of the Fako Section of the Cameroon National Union, Dr. E. M. L. Endeley and the Minister of Mines and Energy, Mr. Philemon Yang. The climax of the ceremony was the cutting of the tape, the unveiling of a memorial plaque, and the brief tour of the refinery installations.

Ndumbe's problem at this stage was how he could get his truck to the refinery. He had arrived late and had to park his vehicle two kilometres from the refinery. Ngowo had cleverly avoided marching with the other women. She had discovered that they did not bring any jugs with them!

The crowd had now started to disperse. Ndumbe decided he would join the group of invitees which moved towards the restaurant for the buffet luncheon. There was a long queue and he observed the protocol and security officers were checking the invitations as the queue moved on. But he had heard that it was a free-for-all luncheon! And he had received no invitation! He was a militant like the rest of them! Or was he in the wrong queue? He looked around again. Every invitee had an invitation card. He decided he would avoid the embarrassment of being turned back. He would rather withdraw honourably than face the rebuff which was now inevitable.

'Excuse me,' he said to the couple behind him, and retreated. He walked by the administrative block. There were a lot of security officers on crowd control duty. Ndumbe joined the jostling throng. He tried to look back at the queue he had just left. 'Heh you there, you are obstructing. Will you get moving? And quick!' The policeman was pointing at him. He moved on wondering why the officer had picked on him.

Ngowo still carried the empty twenty-litre jug wondering when the tanks would be opened for her to fill her jug with wine. 'Get moving there, you with your jug.' The policeman had been watching her for some time. It was the source of some fun for everyone looked in her direction. How embarrassed she felt. Why on earth should she be carrying an empty jug, and on this day of days! She walked briskly away.

She would give her husband a good telling off for making such a fool of her.

Later that evening, she waited for his return. He arrived late looking tired and hungry and without the car. 'Look, what happened,' he began apologetically. 'They did not fill the car with petrol after all. I have had to come back on foot. I ran out of petrol on my way back.' Ngowo burst into uncontrollable peals of laughter until her sides ached and the tears coursed down her cheeks. 'Serves you right.' Ndumbe just looked at his wife. 'I am hungry,' he said simply. 'There was no free-for-all luncheon after all.' 'But everything went on so well and it did not rain after all,' Ngowo added as she laid the table.

'Wait a minute,' her husband said moving towards the bedroom. He returned with a burning hurricane lantern. 'These people cannot eat their cake and have it. They will have to attend the inauguration ball in the rain!' Ndumbe blew the flame with his breath. The flame flickered and went out. A few minutes later came the patter of rain drops on the roof. It rained and rained and rained, and the wind lashed and lashed and lashed.

Trial by Ordeal

It all happened in a small workers' camp. The population was about four hundred all told. This included the wives and children. Four long rows of corrugated iron-roofed labour lines, a small community hall, two pit latrines and wash houses some distance away, a workers' shop and the estate office. An eighteen-inch-gauge rail line circumvented the camp in a north-easterly direction towards the Estate Manager's house – an old German bungalow perched on cement stilts. A peaceful little community in tidy and clean surroundings, away from the hustle and bustle of the town, some ten kilometres away. The labourers nicknamed the place 'Small London'. It had lost its original name. The Germans had called it 'Keta Plantation'. They were very proud of Small London and its daily routine – wake up, go work, come chop, drink mimbo and tory, dance small and sleep.

The drum beats had as usual roused the little sleepy community. It was 5.30 a.m. – time for roll call. The time-keeper virtually barked the names on his time book over the loud chattering that was going on. He stopped time and again to let the clang, clang of buckets and tapping knives die down.

The roll call had always amused him. Like the labourer who was known simply as 'Money Hard' who always indicated his presence by answering 'Woman no Sabi'. Like Mr. 'Time for Tro' too who merely shouted 'I never die'. It raised a lot of laughter. It was the same on pay day.

After the roll call, the tappers went on their rounds, the clearing gangs were allocated plots or lines to clear, while the processing-gang left for the factory to begin processing the previous day's latex then in coagulating tanks.

Ngwa, rubber tapper on Plot EE 110, had a problem on his mind. He needed a pair of new rubber boots. The toes were already sticking out of the old ones and he had no money left to buy a new pair. But he had always found a solution when he found himself so hard up. He had taken the money off someone and had got away with it. Sometimes he wondered why no notice had been taken of the petty thefts he had indulged in. His thoughts wandered as he went through the last twenty trees to complete his daily task.

He reckoned it would be a simple operation. After all, he had become a professional thief! That window was always left open, he thought, as he emptied his last bucket of latex at the collecting station. He walked back quickly to the camp with the plan clearly in his mind.

The camp was quiet when he arrived. He was the first worker to complete his task. He thought the timing ideal for his plan. The women were away in their farms and market. The older children had gone to school too. The Camp was virtually deserted except for a group of naked children who were busy playing in the dust.

The door was not locked. He pushed it open, entered and went straight to the bamboo bed. He raised the pillow, then the raffia mat! There was the money he wanted – five pounds! He picked the money and shoved it inside the right boot. He then moved to the door, opened it slowly, looked this way and that. There was no one in sight. He stepped out and walked back to his room.

Samba, Secretary of the 'Njangi' Group, had received contributions from ten members at the end of the month. They had each contributed ten shillings. They had arranged to meet in the Community Hall to hand over the money to the recipient. Light refreshments had been provided from the entertainment fund. These included soya, groundnuts, cooked pieces of stock fish and fresh palm wine. Samba had also prepared a receipt for the recipient to sign.

He looked at his watch. It was ten minutes to four o'clock. He had to get there on time to collect a fine of three pence from late-comers. The meeting time was four o'clock prompt. He raised the pillow and the mat. There was no money. He tore down the mosquito net, took the broom and swept all the corners of the room diligently. No money. A wave of panic swept through him as he searched the room feverishly. Who could have removed the money? It was not his money. What explanation would he give to the other members of the group? Would they believe his story? He had

11

to act quickly. He should report the incident to the Camp Warden. He would at this time be supervising the disposal of garbage by one of the clearing gangs. He would try the dumping-site first. He was completely out of breath when he at last found him.

'Now, what's wrong Samba? You have been running!' 'Ma–ma–s–s–sa, I– I– don d–d–ie,' he stammered. The other man looked at him in surprise and tried to calm him. 'Now, Samba, what is it? Now take your time.'

'Massa, I tell you say, I don die. Tief-man don kill me. Five pong, don go. Na "Njangi" money, no bi my money. Whetin I go do?' He broke down and started sobbing.

This was not the first complaint Mr. Mba had received about the growing incidence of thefts in Small London. The subject had been discussed at the weekly meeting of Supervisors presided over by the Estate Manager. It had been decided that extra labourers be detailed on the dual duties of refuse disposal and general surveillance. The police were to be invited to conduct their investigations of cases of theft which came to light – measures intended to curb the activities of thieves within the Estate Community.

When the anguish, nervousness and excitement had died down, Samba recounted the story of the missing five pounds. He had hidden the money under the mat – money he had collected as Secretary of the 'Njangi' Group. Someone had stolen the money. Mr. Mba listened to the story without interrupting the speaker. He later asked a few questions and decided he would report to his Estate Manager.

Stan Williams, the Estate Manager, listened to the story with a deepening frown. He finally got up and started pacing the room with his hands behind his back. This was a habit of his – he was thinking. He stopped for a while, staring at the rubber trees through the open window. Then he turned round and faced the Camp Warden. 'Do you suspect any one?' 'No, Sir,' he replied. 'Any stranger seen around the camp when the workers were at work?' 'No, Sir, I have received no such information. It must be someone among the workers. I am convinced, Sir.' The Camp Warden emphasized the last sentence.

'Right, beat the drum, I'd like to talk to the people. Just now, savvy?' The warden walked down the office steps to the wooden drum. He took the drum-sticks. The sound of the drum broke the stillness of the afternoon. The men lounging and others playing cards, ludo and draughts in the Community Hall, looked up in the direction of the office wondering what it was all about. Even the kids playing in the dust greeted the drum-beats with whoops of excitement. A crowd of anxious workmen later listened to their Estate Manager.

'I have called you all here, to talk to you. This is about the limit. We have had too much 'tiefing' in this camp of late. Too many bad people. Plenty "teif-man" de for Small London. No good at all, at all. Bring plenty shame, eh! If there is anyone among you here who can give any information, it will be taken in confidence. There should be no fear. This "tief-man" must be caught and dealt with by the law. "Tief-man" must return money tomorrow, otherwise police come.' The address was short and blunt. It left the assembly restless. The atmosphere became tense as the Manager left the gathering. He conferred with the Camp Warden and finally departed.

Who among them was the thief? Who among them had brought shame to Small London? Who among them was the black sheep? The crowd was hushed. The warden was going to speak. 'You all know what has happened – the Manager has already told you. This is a very bad thing. Too much. One among us is the thief. The Manager has given three days and unless the money is returned, the whole of "E" line will be terminated. The workers will collect their last pay including two weeks notice-pay and gratuity for those who have served five years and over. Nine days will be given for the workers to leave the estate or face forcible eviction. I hope you realise what this means. It means that for the 'bad fashion' of one man, other workers including their wives and children will suffer. That is why I am asking that we should leave no stone unturned to catch this tief-man. Any man like for talk some thing?' He stopped and surveyed the crowd. Someone raised his hand. 'Yes, Fineboy,' the warden pointed in his direction. There was some acclamation from the workers. Fineboy had

on many occasions arrogated to himself the role of spokesman for the camp community. There was silence as he raised
his hand.

'My brothers and country people,' he began. 'I think say, we
all for here just now, agree say tief na bad thing. No bi so?'
The crowd answered 'Yes' in unison. 'Alright, I want sabi if
we go agree say make we all suffer with we woman and pikin
because of one tief-man.' The crowd shouted 'No'. 'Me, I
think say we go call that Ngambi-man for Motoke for cam
here for camp for proof this tief-man. No bi so?' 'Na so–o–o,'
the crowd answered. Fineboy turned to the warden. 'I think
say massa fit go tell manager say na so all people for camp
talk.' There were shouts of approval and clapping from the
crowd. The meeting broke up.

Mr. Mba had reported the decision of the workers to the
Manager. He had pointed out how difficult it was to replace
all the workers in 'E' Line, who were, according to his
estimation, very efficient rubber tappers. He convinced the
manager of the juju-man's powers. He said the man had been
called on some similar incident. Some Government Treasury
Cashier had stolen a large sum of money and had hidden the
haul in a hole in the bush. The money was found intact – not
a penny had been spent! Unorthodox though it appeared,
Stan yielded. He had been advised many a time not to dismiss
African beliefs and customs with contempt, however ridiculous and superstitious they appeared at first in European
eyes.

News of the impending trial by ordeal had spread throughout the neighbourhood and there was a very large crowd of
anxious and expectant workers waiting in the sun outside the
Community Hall. Everyone waited to witness this unusual
occurrence. There was a lot of jostling and shuffling when the
juju-man arrived closely followed by a boy of seven who
carried a bulging raffia-bag slung over his shoulder.

The man wore a piece of loin-cloth which he bunched
around his waist, a black double-breasted coat and an old
battered hat. He ignored the Estate Manager and his group,
which included the Camp Warden and Fineboy who had
made the contacts. He walked towards the entrance into the

hall. It had been arranged that nobody should enter the hall before he did. He entered the hall, looked around and returned. Then he retrieved the raffia bag and took out what looked like an ordinary piece of fibre-rope. He put it down on the ground across the door. Only the residents of Small London were to go into the Hall. One by one they filed into the hall in silence stepping over the piece of rope.

What would happen to him if he stepped over the rope like the rest? Ngwa wondered as he filed behind the other residents of Small London. A slight ripple of fear went through him. Why had he come after all? He could have kept away without attracting any attention. Stupid of him not to have thought of that! It was too late now to get away. It was his turn now. He stepped over the rope, his heart beating a fast tattoo as he did. Nothing happened! He walked into the hall with the rest of them – including the Estate Manager.

The juju-man was the last to enter. He picked up the rope, holding it away from him as if he feared some contamination! He stopped in the centre of the hall, made a few clockwise turns and dropped the rope on the floor. He then emptied his bag and arranged an array of objects which included little carved and hideous-looking figures smeared with what looked like blood, cowrie shells, little mirrors, candles, bottles of perfume, various concoctions and the odd bits found among the paraphernalia of witch-doctors and seers. He then stood up and faced the crowded hall. He said that long ago there were no courts as we had today. The dispensation of justice then was most effective. It was swift and without fear or favour – no evidence, witnesses or lawyers. What he had been called to do was what his forefathers did before him – to smell-out the tief-man.

Having said so, he picked up a number of rings which he dutifully slid over the fingers of both hands and took one of the perfume bottles. He sprayed the perfume over the array of objects before him, applied some on his palms and rubbed his face. He brought out eight cowrie shells from his pocket, spat on them and threw them on the floor before him. He stared at them for some time, gathered them in his right hand and threw them down again.

15

He then recited some unintelligible jargon and broke into a chant. He called on the Fako Mountain, the god of his fathers and the spirits of the living and the dead. He prayed them to open the way. 'Tell me,' he said, raising both hands above his head, 'who is the bad man, the man among us who is the thief.' Suddenly there came a series of chirps, the type produced by crickets, from the array of objects before him. His face lightened and he laughed. 'Is the thief in this hall?' he asked. The chirping came on again. 'And you will let us see him?' There was a long drawn chirp and out rolled a fluffy ball wrapped with red and black cloth.

The crowd watched spellbound as the object rolled towards the crowded hall, chirping. Some of the people moved away as it progressed, followed closely by the juju man. When it did stop, it was between Ngwa's feet. Ngwa's eyes goggled in utter disbelief as he stared incredulously at the ball. He loudly protested his innocence, but the juju-man had not finished with him. He said the money was hidden in Ngwa's room in the camp.

A long procession led by the little boy clasping the ball in his cupped hands walked to the camp. The boy seemed possessed as he walked slowly, staggering sometimes. He stopped when he came to 'E' Line and pointed to a door. It was Ngwa's room. He was asked to lead the way, followed by the little boy, the juju-man, the Estate Manager and his group. After a few preliminaries the juju-man asked one of the men to lift the earthen-pot which contained drinking water. It was lifted, and there to everyone's surprise were the missing five pound notes. The crowd gave way as Ngwa was taken away, the Estate Manager displaying the money as they progressed through the crowd. There were shouts of 'Tief-man!, tief-man!' as they took away Ngwa and the children took up the song, clapping their hands as they sang:

Tiefy Tiefy	*Jankaliko*
Jankaliko	*Five pong*
I no de shame	*Jankaliko*
Jankaliko	*Ole-ole*
I tief money	*Jankaliko*

God of Meme

The villagers named the festival the 'Visitation'. A festival handed down by their grandfathers and great-great-grandfathers before them. Once a year, they assembled on the banks of the Mungo River, to pay homage and sing praises to the 'god' of the river.

They had trekked for miles, men, women and children. Among the throng were members of the man-crocodile cult, identified by woven strands of crocodile-hide worn around their right ankles.

Members of the cult were held in great respect and awe. There were the stories of the fanatic adherence to the cult by its members; its survival under the ruthlessness of the early German administrators, and its near demise as a result of the persuasions and organised campaigns by the Christian missionaries.

The crowd retreated as members of the cult trooped down the riverbank; two of them carrying a bleating he-goat for the sacrifice, another followed with a matchet. The ceremony was brief. The goat was tethered on to a stake driven into the ground. They then surrounded the goat – all of them. The tallest of them raised the matchet high above his head, then brought it down – one stroke that severed the head from the body. The blood-spattered carcass was flung deep into the river.

Then the drumming, singing and clapping started, with members of the cult performing a jig peculiar only to their group. One of their members had worked himself into a frenzy as the tempo of the drumming increased and dropped heavily on the ground. His colleagues quickly cordoned off the area, rallying round him as he lay sprawled on the ground, quite relaxed, his chest heaving slowly. The rest continued in hilarious mood, stamping their feet as the drums throbbed louder and louder.

From the opposite bank of the river came a loud snort, then the snout, the large protruding eyes, the head and the long-scaly body.

17

The crowd yelled in ecstacy and prayed in unison –

Lord of the river
Thy might we acknowledge
Protect us from the evil one
Fill the bellies of our women with babies
And provide the rich harvest to feed them
Long may you reign

The crocodile waddled up the opposite bank and opened its mouth in greeting, displaying two long rows of gleaming white teeth. The crowd roared and cheered hysterically as it later submerged, retrieved the carcass, thrashed its tail and glided slowly downstream and out of sight.

The crocodiles in this river were docile beasts – domesticated, to be more exact. They could be identified, talked to and stroked lovingly. I myself had witnessed a startling and weird incident while taking a trip by canoe to one of the villages. We had come across what appeared to be a log of timber. The canoe-man had tried to manoeuvre his craft on course, when a member of the cult, who happened to be travelling with us, ordered him to drop anchor. He announced, rather jokingly that a friend of his had blocked our course. He then stood up, waved his hands in salute and called: 'Lokindo . . . lokindo . . . Masengo, your colleague, salutes you. Pray let us proceed.' A few yams were thrown overboard, and what had appeared to the rest of us as a log of timber turned out to be a live crocodile. It thrashed its tail, submerged, and gave us right of way.

Many a time, the crocodiles lay basking in the sun on the muddy bank while men, women and children swam and bathed with no concern whatsoever regarding their safety. They all knew the animals were harmless – human beings in crocodile form. The story goes, however, that a certain German administrator, named Von Schnieder, had been killed by a crocodile. That he was the only victim seized from a group of five. The rest were unharmed. They said it was a reprisal for his brutality and other acts of callousness against the natives. They said he had caused ten identified members of the man-crocodile cult be shot.

The natives around had been summoned forcibly at gun-point to witness what was classified as a punitive measure. In a specially prepared arena, the condemned men were made to climb on trees and a game hunting exercise began. White soldiers armed with rifles brought them down one by one – a spectacle that was intended to shock the natives into submission. Those who showed signs of sympathy or wept for executed relatives or friends were stripped and whipped with horse-whips. Von Schnieder's corpse was never found.

But the 'god' of the river was now ageing. He had lost his youthful skill and speed that had earlier characterised the quick despatch of his victims. He had been content with lying in wait for forest animals – antelopes and other small game which came down regularly for a drink. Many a time he had succeeded in flailing them with his powerful scaly tail, so powerful that it crushed the victim into a battered shuddering heap. The strong jaws and claws retracted into the body which was then dragged virtually under water and drowned.

Today, he had watched a small herd of antelopes cropping the grass, anxious for water, but for some reason he did not know, afraid to approach the river. He moved slowly. Only the tip of the snout and the large bulging eyes above water.

Two young antelopes ventured down the river's edge. They seemed to have sensed the danger, for they suddenly stopped drinking, raised their heads and cocked their ears. Now, he must take his time. A lot depended on this particular kill – he had been some days without food. He made a desperate dash for the nearest antelope. His timing was faulty, and he had just missed his victim by inches. The animals gave the alarm and the whole herd stampeded to the safety of the forest.

Further up the river, a little footpath zig-zagged to the river bank. The local people simply called the place 'Small Beach'. Here, everyone to and from the village had to be taken across by canoe. It was market day, a very busy day for the canoe-man. Women with baskets of cocoyams and plantains strapped on their backs stood waiting for their turn. Today, they were growing rather impatient and angry – the canoe-man had arbitrarily raised the toll by two pence.

The 'god' of the river watched these goings and comings with renewed interest. Not that he was doing so for the first time. Today he was hungrier than usual; really hungry and the urge to survive had put him in a different frame of mind. He wondered what human flesh tasted like. 'Must be horrible,' he thought as he tried to work out how best he would set about it. It was a strange feeling that touched his very heart, but the urge to survive was uppermost.

Five more persons had arrived – three women carrying baskets of cassava on their heads and two petty-traders on bicycles. Two of the women were first taken across; the third had emptied her basket of cassava and started peeling them. The two men with the bicycles were ferried across too, and finally the broad-breasted woman, who had by now finished peeling her cassava. After taking her across, the canoe-man settled down to his breakfast of koki and plantain. After the meal, he walked down to the river to rinse his mouth and wash his hands.

There was no one in sight. The crocodile moved closer. 'Now, I must take my time,' he thought. Another false movement meant another day without food. He wanted it to be a clean business. None of his subjects should witness such an atrocity. The 'god' of the river was becoming a man-eater.

The man washed his hands, scooped out the water in the boat and checked the mooring rope. Satisfied that all was well, he walked a few paces from the water's-edge and sat down for a brief rest before his customers arrived for the return-trip.

The crocodile moved stealthily closer. He was not sure whether the man's gaze was fixed on the river. It became clear, as he drew closer, that the man was dozing. Then he struck. It was quick work, delivered with the right timing and precision. Only a sharp, muffled scream. The powerful jaws locked on the man's shoulder like a vice and dragged him to the bottom of the river. The now limp body coughed and kicked desperately until it choked and lay still.

The villagers found the bloody trail. The canoe still lay moored. They could not believe their eyes! It had never happened before! They could not understand it at all, and no one dared accuse the 'god' of the river of such an atrocity!

And so the 'god' of the river's blood-lust continued with unabated fury. The baby left by the mother to wander while she did her laundry had disappeared. Villagers paddling down river in canoes laden with cocoyams and plantains had been chased by the crocodile. At first, the smell of human blood had sickened and frightened him. Now it had a sweetness that caused him pangs of desire to kill again and again.

The next victim was Water-boy, the labourer who carried water from the river to the Estate Manager's house up the hill. Once again, it was a successful operation. Only Water-boy's empty bucket was found. There again were the signs the unseen and merciless enemy had left behind – a bloody trail which ended by the river bank.

Following this latest incident, David Jones, the Estate Manager had received a delegation of the Workers' Trade Union. They demanded that some drastic action be taken to safeguard the lives of its members. They had given the Manager ten days to show what was described as some positive measures, failing which the Union would take any action it deemed fit. It was clear to the five-man delegation that the Manager was equally concerned about the recent threat on the peaceful and orderly existence of his little community. He realised that he would have to pay large sums of money under the Workmen's Compensation Ordinance if the crocodile's blood-lust continued.

David Jones had discussed the matter with the local Administrative Officer, suggesting that the man-crocodile cult be banned. He had argued that the crocodile was a menace and its continued existence not conducive to public peace and safety. He was aware that crocodiles were protected under the Wild Life Preservation Ordinance, but there was the proviso which stated that if such protected game threatened the peaceful and orderly existence of the community, thereby constituting a danger to life and property, it could be destroyed in the public interest.

This is why David Jones had shot at the beast when it killed his dog before his very eyes. The livid flash and the explosion had brought down groups of scared and angry villagers, all members of the cult to the river bank. They had protested vehemently and explained that the recent happenings were the wrath of the 'god' of the river. The spokesman pointed out that the tendency had been for certain persons to ignore the laid down taboos with regard to the river. They had continued to shout across the river; they had continued to wash the soot off cooking pots and 'bitter-leaf' in the river. All these actions were regarded and accepted as gross disrespect for the 'god' of the river. His recent attempt to kill the 'god' of the river was an affront and a desecration – an act which was likely to cause a breach of the peace. They wanted an assurance that the 'god' of the river would not be threatened or molested. 'You will be taken away like the other whiteman before you, if you persist,' they warned him.

The meeting ended in uproar. The Manager accused the group of blackmail, asked them out of his office and threatened to call the police. That settled it. They shook their fists and cursed as they backed away. They swore they would 'call' the rain. And the rain came a few hours after the meeting. It rained as it had never rained before. The river began to rise, and twenty-four hours later the young rubber trees were standing in three feet of water. Reports soon came in about the two wooden bridges which had been swept away by the floods. Effective supervision of the estate was now impossible. The rain-makers too had joined the vicious circle.

At the meeting convened by the District Officer to agree to a line of action, the District Clerk, a local man who had made good, sat tight-lipped throughout the discussions. He looked greatly terrified when opinion weighed in favour of shooting the crocodile. He had pleaded in tears that such an act would completely disrupt the communal life of his people. He expressed the fear that he would be killed by a crocodile if it was known that he had connived with the administration in taking such a decision. His fears were allayed. He was promised protection against any possible reprisals or molestation.

But the meeting had not ended when a court messenger arrived with the sad news of yet another victim – a little girl aged ten. Something had to be done at once. The man-eater was to be destroyed and the activities of the cult banned. That was the consensus. Orders were given for four policemen with crack shots to be issued with four rounds of ammunition each. They were to report to headquarters for briefing. A Land Rover equipped with radio communication equipment, tear gas and hand-cuffs was requisitioned in case there was mob-resistance. The little force then left, led by the Administrative Officer and the Police Commissioner.

The road was steep all the way and rugged. There were several flooded stretches and time and again the auxiliary gears had to be engaged. After half an hour the Land Rover chugged to a halt. They had come to the end of the motorable road. The rest of the journey had to be done on foot, through a bush track – a distance of about two miles. The forest was thick, and sometimes it was dark as the dense foliage cut off most of the light.

It was about midday when they arrived at a clearing. The vegetation was less dense. There were plantain and cocoyam farms all over and in the distance there was rising smoke. Another ten minutes trek brought them to the village. It was like every other village in the district – a tight cluster of bamboo huts covered with thatch. There was a large crowd at one end. People were talking in low tones and over the hum of voices came the traditional wailing so common at village funerals.

The crowd moved back slowly as the group arrived. There, on a rough wooden bed, lay the mangled remains of the ten year-old girl. The body had been found with the face torn off and the guts scooped.

A slight rustle commenced among the audience as the policemen unshouldered their rifles. Then there was silence as the voice of authority spoke. 'This is a very sad thing,' the District Officer began. 'Very sad, very bad thing,' he emphasised, picking his words slowly. 'This thing cannot be allowed to go on. People cannot continue to live in fear. Government has an obligation to protect its citizens. This animal is a menace, and it is the Government's determination that it be destroyed.' He stopped and watched the reaction of the

23

crowd. Then he went on. 'I want three powerful men to pull us up the river in a boat.' There was silence. 'Are there no volunteers? I will give you three minutes to decide. Thereafter I will take whatever action I deem fit.'

The villagers stood their ground. None of them wished to be involved in what they considered a conspiracy against the 'god' of the river. The Administrative Officer looked at his watch and raised his hand. 'You, you, and you,' he pointed to three stocky, broad-chested villagers. 'March these fellows down the river.' The policemen stepped forward, their guns held menacingly. The terrified men meekly and resignedly did a 'quick march' as ordered.

One man in the crowd eyed the Administrative Officer owlishly. He began reciting an unintelligible litany of woe, followed by an unending flood of bitter invective. The man was simply known as Tata Maloba, a surly old man aged about sixty. 'And what's the meaning of this?' he screamed, his look glowering – contempt mingled with respect. 'I've come to shoot the rogue of a crocodile and nothing will stop me. I don't even care if it is your own.' He looked determined. The old man threw himself on the ground begging. He would never molest or kill anyone, ever again. He was bluntly told that it was now too late and that his confession could not help him.

Tata Maloba's crocodile lay basking peacefully as a result of the previous day's heavy meal, when the plop-plop of dipping paddles came to him; then the voices of men. His first instinct was to slip away unobserved. But it was too late; the men in the boat had seen him.

Corporal Doh, the man with the best shot, stood up. He withdrew the bolt of his rifle, slid a round into the breech and signed himself. His breathing deepened with nervous excitement as he raised the rifle high in the port, its butt pressing into his armpit. Then he pulled the trigger. He heard the explosion and the short screech of the bullet which smashed into the animal's head. Then followed three other explosions in quick succession as the other men raked him again and again.

The river took on a deeper brown hue as the crocodile in

the throes of death thrashed and churned the muddy waters. It took some time to die, making noises that were really human, with eyes full of hate watching the men in the boat as it died.

Back in the village, a small crowd gathered as Tata Maloba collapsed, screaming and clutching at his head, crying: 'I've been shot . . . I've been shot . . . I'm dying . . .' And he died soon after. The post mortem indeed proved that he had died from gun-shot wounds. The corpse was riddled all over by bullets.

Post Mortem

About three months after Mola Ndive died, I saw his ghost walking along the road leading to the Engelberg Mission School in Bonjongo. It was about 8.30 in the morning as I was hurrying to school. My pencil had dropped through a hole in the pocket of my shirt. I was sure I had put it there when I started off, so I retraced my steps looking and searching the ground before me. I had walked about ten yards when I came face to face with a man carrying a climbing rope over his shoulder. There was no possibility that I was mistaken about who or what I saw. There was Mola Ndive himself in the flesh, very much alive, tall, stoopy and grey haired. He still wore that old bush shirt torn at the back and the striped piece of loin cloth around his waist. This was not a case of mistaken identity, and I'll tell you why.

I was ten years old when it happened and in Standard Four. Mola Ndive was my mother's half-brother, from the same father. He lived a couple of houses away from our home and I saw him everyday when he came for his dinner. He had a swelling, the size of a basket ball between his legs. That ball still hung there. There was no mistake whatsoever about his real identity.

Others had identified him at various times and places. There had been reports of knockings at night in the family house where the widow had been staying until the traditional funeral rites were performed. All these visits were preceded by the endless whining and barking of dogs – a sure sign that something mysterious and weird was around.

Then something else happened. This time the widow had sworn that he walked into the bedroom and asked her to turn over so that they should sleep. Her loud screams for help had aroused the household and the neighbours around the house. She had been so terrified that she clung to the first person who came to her rescue like a frightened child. She had received a terrible shock that kept her temporarily dumb for three days. They had searched in vain – Mola Ndive's ghost had vanished.

Mola Ndive had died from what was clearly a case of strangulated hernia. He had survived a number of mild attacks merely by squeezing the enlarged scrotum. This time the attack was severe and required some emergency operation. Nothing could be done to save him. They would have been obliged to carry him to the local hospital eight miles away on some improvised stretcher made from a piece of bed sheet and two stout poles, through a hilly and difficult terrain. But they had waited too long and he had died.

I remember that he died on a market day. It was getting dark and the village church bell, a four-foot steel railway sleeper struck with a steel rod, broke the stillness of the evening. It was not the successive bong! bong! bong! which summoned the woman's choir – *ndola bito*. It was one 'bong' followed by a break of about thirty seconds, then another 'bong'. My mother stopped pounding the cocoyam foofoo and listened. The 'bongs' continued for quite some time. She put the mortar and pestle away against the wall and left the house; someone had called her. When she returned some minutes later, I sensed that something had gone wrong. She announced briefly that Mola Ndive had died. She cried softly, the tears coursing down her cheeks as she continued pounding the foofoo. My younger sister started whimpering and we both joined mother to share her grief.

She soon realised that she had upset us by having given vent to her feelings and emotion in our presence. She wiped away her tears and assured us that food would soon be ready. We had started eating in silence when an aunt from the neighbouring village arrived. She started wailing the traditional way – tearing away her hair and rolling on the ground. When she entered the house she threw herself onto my mother. They locked themselves in a long embrace and continued to cry, ignoring our presence completely. When the sudden out-burst of grief had subsided, both women sat facing each other and in soft tones, almost reduced to whispers, my aunt recounted Mola Ndive's diabolical activities during his life time.

She said he had been initiated into the famous witch-craft society called '*Nyongo*' and named two young men he had 'killed'. The entire village had come out in protest demanding that he be tried by ordeal. It had taken the village council some time to take a decision. They had finally agreed that he be tried. This was to be a guarded secret. The authorities must not know. The trial by ordeal had been banned by law. This banning had followed reports of a previous trial that resulted in the death of a woman accused of witchcraft. The Germans had in their usual ruthlessness, as the story goes, hanged the witch doctor.

Mola Ndive was to be tried in the presence of the aggrieved families, his own family and the village Community. He had been given a large bowl containing a potion made from sasswood prepared by the *Nganga* or witch doctor. He had survived the ordeal because the family had bribed the administrators who had weakened the potion by diluting it with a lot of water. 'Now they have got him,' she sighed. She went on to reveal that Mola Ndive had confessed his guilt shortly before he died. He was sorry he had brought shame to the family by his diabolical activities. He said he could not help it. He had developed a certain evil urge to 'kill' and 'kill'. He had talked of a large cocoa plantation somewhere in the Kube Plains, where the 'victims' were taken to some sort of slave labour camp. He had explained these 'victims' did not actually die. They were put into some kind of 'deep sleep' or trance. They became docile with no will of their own on arrival at the plantations. They only did what they were told to do – human robots whose new and changed life was to work, work and work.

'And that little boy,' they both looked in my direction. 'I hope no harm comes to him – he loved him so!' They said no more. My mother left the house abruptly, it seemed she had forgotten something. When she returned, almost immediately she brought with her a special little weed which grew around the house. This was tied round our wrists, to prevent Mola Ndive's spirit from lingering around us. We were then taken away with other children of the family to stay with

28

relatives in the neighbouring village until the customary funeral rites were over.

We returned home after the fifth day. I observed that members of the family had shaved the hair on their heads completely and wore black clothes. Mother simply commented that Mola Ndive had gone to meet his father's fathers. We did not understand and asked no questions. The whole matter of death and witchcraft had been shrouded in mystery. There was a fresh mound of earth outside Mola Ndive's house – that was where they had buried him. Around the mound was a lot of torn clothing, an old and frayed black coat, a battered hat, a walking stick and some broken iron-pots and plates. It was believed that Mola Ndive would need all these items to start his new life in the next world. I considered the prospect of Mola Ndive coming back to life for some unknown reason, only to discover that he had been locked in a box six feet below the ground! That would be a terrible thing. No one would hear his cries for help. The thought made me very sad.

The frequent appearances of Mola Ndive's ghost affected the daily lives of the village community. The men had to accompany their wives to their farms. It had been rumoured that Mola Ndive had developed certain vices since his death. That he had become a sex maniac. He had molested his wife on many occasions. The villagers had to retire early to the safety of their homes as the ghost normally started its prowls at nine o'clock. If one had to travel at night one had to carry a burning kerosene lantern. It was believed that ghosts only haunted in the dark and were afraid of lights.

Bonjongo was a village of dark traditions – the only village in the whole clan which still kept a shrine – *Mbando*. The community had to offer some sacrifice from time to time. Like the small pox epidemic of 1921 which took away many lives and left those who survived with pitted and deformed faces. All the adult males and females had turned out naked in the night and paraded through the village admonishing the evil spirits in song.

The village head received a delegation of elders. Some

29

urgent action had to be taken to put Mola Ndive's spirit 'at rest'. They had consulted the 'seer' who told them that they would find a hole by the side of the grave. He said Mola Ndive who came out of his grave in the form of a lizard later transformed himself into the ghost which had continued to haunt the village. And the hole was there! Just as the witch-doctor had said.

A brief ritual was held by the grave side. It included the slaughter of a goat and the blocking of the hole with specially prepared herbs tied up in a small bundle. But Mola Ndive's ghost continued haunting and terrorising the little community. A second visit and inspection of the grave showed that the hole was still there – the little bundle of herbs had disappeared!

On my way to school I had lost my pencil, and while looking for it, I came face to face with Mola Ndive's ghost. I recognised him at once, there was no mistake about it. He brushed past me without a word. I was surprised that he took no notice of me. Then suddenly as I watched spell-bound his figure became blurred and faded away before my very eyes. He just vanished, into thin air.

A moaning gust of cold wind swept past me, putting me in a state of icy horror. Then the skin over my skull tingled with a warmth that left me transfixed and numb. I tried to run but it appeared I was being held down by unseen weights. I tried to shout but felt a violent contriction in my throat. When that queer, eerie feeling finally left me I dashed in the opposite direction, let out a frightened scream that brought everybody out within earshot. 'What's the matter?' 'What's happened?' I could hear them asking. I did not stop. I continued running and soon everyone was running too. Pandemonium had broken loose. I had almost covered the ground and was turning towards our house when an old man hobbled across the way. Then it happened – a collision – millions of twinkling stars then complete darkness.

I found myself in a strange little village much smaller than Longongo. The huts were built of mud and thatch. There were a lot of old men assembled and sitting in a circle. It appeared that a meeting was going on when I arrived. One among the group must have said something for everyone turned round looking in my direction, watching me as I picked my steps hesitatingly. My heart gave a little flutter which raised my hopes for there, in their midst, was Mola Ndive. I recognised him.

Once again, I was transfixed. I stood there like a murderer awaiting the verdict of the jury. There was an argument going on at the time. The principal speaker seemed to have made his point. He argued that I had no reason to come before them for judgement and Mola Ndive's explanation did not appear to have satisfied them. The question was put and after a show of hands followed by a count the speaker walked to me. He gave me a slight-slap on my left cheek and ordered me to go back the way I had come.

I woke up suddenly with a start. I opened my eyes. There was a lot of smoke in the room and many people were standing around, talking in low tones. An elderly man who smelt strongly of tobacco bent over me, as I lay on the ground, stroking my forehead and feet with a broom. There was not enough light in the room but I recognised my mother and the other members of the family. They pushed around anxiously as word went round that I had been revived. I became the centre of attraction – everybody wanted to get my story first hand. I was asked a number of questions which I answered with a very clear recollection of all that had happened to me.

The witch doctor explained later that I had actually visited the land of the dead. My return to the land of the living had been due to the disapproval of the Greater Council of Spirits, which had decided that I was too young to do any useful work on the plantations. Mola Ndive's death had been the result of his refusal to produce a substitute. He had decided to 'turn his back'. Now his ghost had run amok and only a post mortem on the corpse would put it finally to rest. He named another witch doctor from the village of Bomboko, who specialised in exorcising spirits and ghosts.

Then followed a ceremony of pouring libation. The witch doctor prayed to the spirits of his ancestors to protect and guide the little community from the hands of evil. Then the drums were brought in and they all danced until the early hours of the morning.

The village council met a few days later. Also at the meeting was Misole, from the village of Bomboko. His mission was to put Mola Ndive's roving ghost finally to rest. When the meeting ended, a date had been fixed for the operation. It was arranged that Misole would be accompanied by six others who would assist with the digging and hauling up of the coffin.

It was past midnight when the little party arrived at the grave side. All was quiet around except for the weird chanting of the witch doctor and the sound of the muffled gong. One of the men carried a loaded dane gun and a matchet. The others shovels and picks. The last carried the juju-bag and a lighted torch of bamboo fronds.

Misole first encircled the grave with some white powder, drove a rattle-spear into the ground beside the grave and ordered the men to start digging. It was hard work and the shovels changed hands as the digging progressed. Forty-five minutes later they hit the coffin. Two stout ropes were thrown in and they all assisted in hauling the coffin to the surface. It was intact. There was no smell of festering human flesh and its weight indicated that the corpse was still inside.

Misole then took over. He tapped the coffin several times with the spear, chanting as he did so. Then he nodded. The others understood and started opening the lid. It was a grisly, hair-raising affair. There in the coffin was a fresh corpse as it had been laid there three months before, its eyes closed and beads of sweat on the forehead. The flaming torch was brought closer and the body examined. The white handkerchief which was used to hold up the lower jaw to prevent it from gaping had been removed. There was a slight twitching of the skin above the temple. The group gazed in complete horror as the witch doctor addressed the corpse. 'At last we have caught up with you, you son of the devil. Why have you continued to harrass the living? Why have you refused to die? Open those evil eyes, quick,' he commanded. The eyes opened. There was a slight movement amongst those who stood looking. Misole raised his hand and went on: 'Now you

will be destroyed . . . destroyed, and may you sleep for ever.'
He ordered them to take the corpse out of the coffin. They
raised the motionless corpse with its eyes still open and placed
it on the ground beside the grave; and the post-mortem
began.

It was quick work. Two four-inch steel nails were handed to
Misole. 'May these eyes never see again,' he murmured as he
prepared to drive them into both eyes. The corpse's face
twitched up again and there was a slight quivering of the
mouth. Then its mouth opened. 'Don't please don't.' It was a
frightened, hoarse plea. 'Shut up,' the witch doctor ordered.
There were tears mixed with blood as the nails pierced the
eyes. Then he took the cutlass. One straight longitudinal
stroke revealed the heart still beating. 'May the heart of the
evil one never beat again,' he pronounced, as he removed it.
The corpse was then laid in the coffin on its face and shot
through the back with the dane gun. The coffin was lowered
again, and the earth filled in once again.

The group with the witch doctor at the rear, walked back to
the village in silence, their heads straight before them. The
assignment had been carried out. It was a successful post-
mortem. Mola Ndive's ghost never appeared again.

Bid for Freedom

Samson Ngomba, Convict No. 2986600, had been put under strict observation following reports by other inmates that he had gone crazy. He often relapsed into great fits of laughter for no apparent cause. There were other moments when he appeared to be preoccupied and moody.

The prison authorities naturally showed some concern for he had, until then, been a well-behaved prisoner – soft-spoken, obedient, reliable.

There were his moments of inspiration, for instance, when he assumed the role of a politician on the soap-box. 'Comrades, Militants, lend me your ears. I stand for Unity, Truth and Democracy. United we stand, divided we fall.' This was his stock introduction which brought shouts of 'Hear, Hear' from his colleagues who found great pleasure and fun in listening to him. It was clear, as the piece of oratory warmed up, that he had been studying the Charter and Constitution of the Cameroon National Union. 'We are going to make this country a great nation,' he continued, raising his clenched fist. 'A prosperous nation that will be the pride of Africa and the world. Towards this end, we shall strive to fight against tribalism and all forms of political strife. We shall encourage the establishment of solidarity and brotherhood between all Cameroon citizens.'

The applause by the audience almost raised the roof. There were shouts of 'Good Talk, Good Talk.' Then he rounded off by leading the group in song. He called it the Freedom Song. A song, which he said, was originally written by a leading Nigerian Politician, Mazi Mbonu Ojike, alias 'Boycott King', of blessed memory.

It ran thus:

Freedom for you, Freedom for me,
Everywhere there must be Freedom,

Chorus:
Freedom, Freedom,

Everywhere there must be Freedom.

Ngomba provided very good entertainment. It greatly
relieved some of the mental strain and boredom so common
with prisoners. In the end, they agreed he talked a lot of
sense. They felt so sorry for him! But he was like the rest of
them – thieves, murderers, terrorists – an enemy of society.

Ngomba was serving a twenty-year jail sentence for embez-
zling public funds – a sum just under a million francs. He
remembered with great regret the circumstances involving
the misappropriation. His friend, the money doubler, had let
him down. Monique and Marylse, the two girls he had given
such a wonderful time! His regular week-end visits to Douala!
Tears rolled down his wasted cheeks as he saw himself in the
dock before the judge passed sentence. The pathetic scene
around the court buildings. A sympathetic crowd watched as
the police led him away.

How angry he felt with himself! He thought of the helplessness and insecurity of the young wife he had left behind. The
thought of who was making love to her while he had been
away filled his heart with jealousy. Twenty years was a long
time! Would she remain faithful? He dismissed the painful
thought from his mind and found great consolation at the
thought of a Presidential Amnesty in commemoration of the
Tenth Anniversary of Cameroon Independence.

The visiting Medical Officer who called at the Prison Sick-
Bay on his weekly rounds spent twenty minutes with
Ngomba, but found nothing wrong with him. Ngomba had
told Dr. Stewart he had dreamt that the President of the
Republic had signed a decree granting him pardon and saw
no reason for his continued detention. He swore Radio
Yaounde had carried an announcement containing the text
of the Presidential Decree and that his name was first on the
list. He went on to quote sections of the Cameroon National
Union Charter and Constitution concerning the liberty of the
individual and the fundamental liberties embodied in the
Universal Declaration of Human Rights.

Dr. Stewart listened patiently to the tirade, nodding approval and showing signs of interest. His diagnosis was brief –

two sentences. 'A passing infatuation. Will get over it'.

But as 1st January 1970 drew near, it was clear from the prisoner's frequent bouts of over enthusiasm, that his desire for freedom had become an obsession. He had started a count-down which only increased his anxiety about the timing of his release from prison.

He had had an argument with the warder the previous day. Ngomba had told the warder he would never set his feet again in prison. 'Don't bluff yourself,' the warder had sneered. 'You will be in here again within a year. You are a thief, you just remember that. A thief, always a thief, and you're nothing different.'

'I am no thief,' he protested. 'Someone played a mean trick on me.' 'How many times have I heard that in here?' the warder laughed. 'Too many times, old boy, and they always complain that they had done nothing wrong! Good luck to you and may your dreams about the Presidential Amnesty come true.'

How unkind of him to have said that to him, Ngomba sighed as he went about his work, his face clouded with sorrow. He had discovered that the prison was not a good place and was determined never to break the law again. Many thoughts flitted through his mind but one was uppermost: 1st January 1970 was just a week ahead and he had heard nothing!

"When am I getting out of this horrible place?' he had asked the warder again one morning. 'You've still a long way to go, my friend. And that cock and bull story about your release. You just get that out of your head,' he added mockingly.

'But I tell you I heard it,' he interrupted. 'I dreamt about it. My old man gave me the tip in my sleep. And you cannot continue to keep me here.' His voice became agitated. The warder looked at the prisoner in surprise. His outburst was unprovoked and he could see the devil in his eyes. He made a report of the incident to the Prison Superintendant. He was convinced that the prisoner was 'funny' in the head. Following his report and investigation, a decision was taken at the daily staff meeting that Ngomba should be placed in solitary confinement. He had a considerable influence over the other inmates and trouble had to be avoided at all costs. From then on, he was referred to as 'Joseph the Dreamer'.

In his solitary confinement, Ngomba planned his escape. If the Prison Authorities decided to defy a Presidential Order to release him, he would take the initiative and bear the consequences. He was going to celebrate Cameroon's Tenth Anniversary of Independence outside the prison walls. He knew it was then or never! Here was his chance and he was going to take it.

It was midnight. All was quiet around except for the loud snoring noises from the adjoining room. Ngomba groped about in the dark on all fours and tip-toed towards the door. Then he stopped suddenly. He thought he heard the heavy plod-plod of booted footsteps on the other side. The fear of being caught frightened him and he darted back to safety. He was just out of earshot, when the door opened throwing a broad beam of light in its wake. There was the silhouette of the warder on duty. A few moments later the door closed again. Ngomba recovered from his fright and prepared himself for the assault on the high wall. His breath came in short gasps as he hauled himself over the nine foot red brick wall and dropped into the bushes on the other side.

It was a long drop that had driven the wind out of his lungs. He felt a stinging pain in his right leg as he lay there for a while, his heart beating a fast tattoo against his chest. Only the slight breeze moving the long elephant grass and the thin piping of a night owl met his anxious ears. There was no sound beyond the wall.

He was free at last! Not only that. He had the head start which he had been counting on. He congratulated himself as he struck for the tall elephant grass in the distance. So long as Lyonga will be there to meet him, everything would be alright. He would be safely in hiding in Douala by tomorrow.

Here he was making history. The first prisoner ever to escape successfully from the local prison. Tomorrow the newspapers would be filled with the story of his escape. There was sure to be a radio announcement alerting the local population, photograph of himself in the papers and the

37

offer of a reward for any information that would lead to his capture.

Other prisoners had gone that far, but in the end hunger and fatigue had proved their pursuers' ally and the end had been in sight before the net had closed in on them. They had been caught running wildly in the bush having lost their bearings, their only objective to put as much distance between them and the prison.

Would this happen to him? he thought as he ran. He had perhaps, half an hour before his escape would be discovered. The telephone wires would soon spread the news and he was sure the police would also be alerted and set up their road blocks.

He reached the tall elephant grass some three hundred yards from the prison wall and plunged into the thick undergrowth. He had been accustomed to the lie of the land during his work with the outside 'gang' which cut and gathered the tender elephant grass for the cows and piglets. And now that he came to think of those cold mornings with only the baggy white shorts, the 'jumper' and the skull-cap on, he hoped his troubles would not be in vain!

The elephant grass and thorn bushes cut his legs viciously and time and again he stumbled onto his knees. He did not feel the wounds. There was no time to waste. The minutes were precious and he strove to maintain the terrific pace he had set himself.

He soon arrived at a small clearing in the bush near the road leading to the village he'd always walked through with the outside gang. Yes, that was the spot, he thought, as he edged his way cautiously towards the little road. Would Lyonga fail him? Fear gripped him at the thought. Would he be there as they'd arranged with the taxi to whisk him off to safety? He was the important link in the chain. A snap and he was finished. His fears were soon allayed, for there it was – he could see the dark lines of a Peugeot saloon car parked in the shadows. As arranged, there came the glow of a smoking cigarette and three short hoots which gave the ALL CLEAR.

Ngomba edged his way cautiously to the car. He gave a little startled gasp. Then his face lit up as he swung round. 'So you managed it!' He almost screamed with joy. 'I told you I'd make it, didn't I?' he replied with great relief. 'Well, it will be fine as long as you use your brains and don't make any mistakes,' Lyonga warned. 'There is every hope of giving your pursuers the final slip.' 'Have you got the things?' he asked looking a bit impatient. 'There is no time to waste'. The other nodded, pointing to the back of the car. A few minutes later the prison clothes were gone and standing in front of Lyonga was a slim and tall female of doubtful age, in a nice fitting frock and head tie.

'Do you really think you can get away with that?' Lyonga eyed him doubtfully.

'I've spent a lot of time thinking this out you know. There is no reason for any anxiety,' he assured him. 'They will be looking for a man and not a woman. You see what I mean, don't you?'

'As long as you always remember you are a woman and behave like one, all will be well. Now quick, let's be off.' The car broke the stillness of the night as it roared down the road trying to avoid the potholes only to fall into them. The plan had been to enable Ngomba to take the first train for a destination where he could lie low until the hue and cry had died down.

At the Douala Central Railway Station, he was buying a ticket when he spotted a policeman standing at the other end of the platform. He eyed the policeman cautiously from the corner of his eye, as he started walking up in his direction. Ngomba drew a deep breath, thanked the ticket clerk in a high falsetto voice, and walked elegantly on to the platform in the opposite direction. He seemed to feel the policeman's eyes on him.

Suddenly the ripple of fear threatened to become a wave of panic. He suddenly thought of the toilets. Yes, that would be a safe place to hide until the train was ready to leave.

With small short steps, he made his way along the platform, went through the doorway and closed the door behind him. Feverishly, he checked on his head-tie, wiped the perspiration from his face and neck.

Then the distant hooting of the train came to him. He

opened the door, walked hurriedly on to the platform and bumped straight into the grim-looking policeman.

'Pardon,' Ngomba apologised as he tried to brush past him.

'Excusez-moi, madame,' the Policeman said politely. 'Maïs pourriez-vous m'accompagner au bureau du Chef de Gare. J'aimerais vous parler.' 'I must catch the train' he waved his hand in urgent protest. But the policeman did not budge. He was pointing, this time, above the doorway Ngomba had just come through. 'Vous voyez, Alors!'

Ngomba looked up at the notice and his heart sank. The doorway was clearly marked MESSIEURS.

The police officer warned his Chef de Gare about the incident in the toilets and reminded him about the message received from Buea about a runaway prisoner. The woman, he said, looked too masculine for a woman; she did not have much of a bust and no 'back-side' at all.

Ngomba grew nervous as he sat down before the scrutinising eyes of the Chef. 'Why had she entered the men's toilet when the two entrances were clearly marked MESDAMES and MESSIEURS?' That was the question. She replied, and quite rightly too, that she could not read French. 'And I lost my father only last week; that's why I shaved all the hair on my head,' she added pitifully, taking off the head-scarf for him to see. The Chef looked at her in surprise. Who had asked her why she had shaved her hair! Then the thought came to him. He invited the woman police officer on duty to his office. 'We wish to establish her real identity,' he pointed at the visitor. 'There's something funny and mysterious about her. Will you take her with you?' The police woman looked puzzled. The Chef observed her bewilderment and quickly added: 'Search her thoroughly, will you?' The police woman noted the emphasis on the word 'thoroughly'; that was exactly what she was going to do.

The Hold-Up Fiasco

It was a very busy Friday morning for the cashiers of the Cameroon Peoples Bank, Douala. It was so at the end of every month, and more so the last banking day before the week-end! Today, the bank was crowded with civil servants who had come from far and near to collect their monthly salaries. The cashiers read the names from a collection of pay slips and handed them over to their respective claimants, who took them and scrutinised them discreetly.

Some of the faces brightened up – others became clouded. There were those the computer had continued to pay months after they had resigned and taken up employment elsewhere. There were those whose pay-packets had doubled for no apparent reason – some unexplained arrears.

For others, the computer had simply not paid. The pay slips showed a list of figures and monies retained or deducted and the balance simply showed zero. Robert Ndumbe viewed the scene before him with sympathy and concern. There was the pregnant woman in tears. For five months it had been the same – the computer had short-paid her. There was the recipient of a cheque that had 'bounced'. There was the man who had misplaced his identity card and could not take his salary and the ensuing argument and protests which he eventually lost.

Ndumbe was growing a bit impatient. He had put in his cheque an hour before. They had stamped it and sent it for verification. One hour had gone and they had told him nothing! He had heard complaints about the growing slackness of the employees of the bank in dealing promptly with customers. He knew his account was 'good' – there was no question whatever of his account being in the 'red'. He had put in a cheque for six million francs. He had been so angry that he had asked to see the General Manager. He had been told there was a long list of customers who wished to see the General Manager and that he had to await his turn.

'What the hell!' he protested. 'How can I wait for two hours

41

to get a cheque of six million francs paid by your bank! I'll have to close my account with your bank, that's all. C'est incroyable. Mon Dieu!'

Everyone in the bank turned to the direction of the speaker, who continued to gesticulate to drive his point home. There was some commotion within the interior of the bank as a search was mounted to trace the cheque. The cheque was later found. An embarrassed General Manager himself left his posh air-conditioned office to apologise for what he called 'an error of judgment'. He later invited Ndumbe to his office, offered him coffee and biscuits and while doing so, ordered the cashier to bring the money into his office. The Manager himself assisted Ndumbe in checking the six million francs in 10.000 francs notes and later locked them up in his brown leather brief-case.

What a fuss he had made. And they had succumbed to it! Well, he had taught them a lesson they would never forget. They should learn to treat customers like himself with some expedition. He would not, after all, withdraw all his money from the bank, he had decided as the General Manager escorted him out of his office. 'Sorry about all that trouble, Mr. Ndumbe, I shall investigate today's incident. I assure you it will never happen again. Please do call again and come straight into my office to see me next time. No formalities.' The Manager smiled affably. They then shook hands.

Two men had watched Ndumbe closely from the moment he entered the bank. They had a clearly defined mission. Today, their venue of operation was the Cameroon Peoples Bank, Douala. They had been checking and observing the customers as they came and went. They were not interested in the civil servants as they considered their salaries 'chicken feed.' They were looking for the tycoons, the big businessmen who banked and withdrew large sums of money. It was easy to recognise them and today they had decided, with the connivance of the bank employee to concentrate on Ndumbe.

One of the two men in dark glasses and peak-cap fixed his gaze on the bank employee who was now attending to Ndumbe. He took the cheque, stamped it and passed it on for verification. Then he looked in the direction of the two men, gave a graceful nod and the thumbs-up sign. They understood. One of them walked to the counter and the employee slipped a piece of paper through the pigeon-hole. The other collected it and left. It was brief message conveying vital information – *Robert Ndumbe. Businessman. Destination Victoria. Withdrew 6.000.000 francs.* They understood. They conferred briefly and one of them left the bank.

Outside the bank, a taxi was waiting. In it were two others. The message was passed on and the strategy planned. Ndumbe was to be accosted politely by the driver immediately he stepped out of the bank. The rest were to keep in the background. It was probable that he would prefer to hire a taxi to take him direct to Victoria. In that case the second taxi with the rest of the group would follow discreetly shadowing the other taxi wherever it went, even if it meant going to Victoria.

In Douala it was a simple operation. The city was big. It was easy to turn into some out of the way place on some little pretext like collecting a forgotten identity card, throw the passenger out of the taxi forcibly with the threat of death and make away with the loot. Victoria would pose a problem. It was a small town where visitors and strangers were easily identified and where mob-justice was very much practised.

With six million francs at stake, the group decided to go on in spite of the many risks involved.

Robert Ndumbe, thirty-six years old, was doing well as a customs clearing agent. Hard work, honesty and the ability to get on with people, were his greatest assets, which he in turn exploited to the fullest. Conversant with customs procedures and regulations, tariffs and, most important of all, his very good relations with the top to bottom customs hierarchy, he was capable of bulldozing his way where his competitors in the same field failed. Importers came all the way from Douala, Bafoussam and Bamenda to get their importation problems solved. He had, in time, developed a flourishing little business based in Victoria.

Ndumbe stepped out of the bank. Instinctively, he clutched his briefcase tightly as if his whole life depended on it. A feeling of insecurity immediately assailed him. He thought of returning to the safety of the bank but decided he would go on. It was about midday. He would like to take his lunch at the Kawa Hotel along the main thoroughfare. He would avoid the out-of-the-way hotels where he was convinced it would be inadvisable to carry around a briefcase containing six million francs. He walked briskly down the steps on to the sidewalk. There was a taxi parked nearby. The driver approached him and asked him politely where he wanted to go. He hesitated for a while, took a quick glance at the man. He did not like his face. 'No, thank you, I prefer to walk.' He walked a few paces and hailed a taxi. 'Kawa Hotel,' he said simply and got into the taxi.

The members of the group who had remained in the background watching as arranged, joined their taxi and started following them. It was getting to the rush hour and the driver of the trailing taxi knew he had to keep fairly close. On one occasion, he beat the traffic lights long after the red light had come on. The traffic policeman on duty was furious, blew his whistle and waved at him to stop. He did not stop. He weaved his way skilfully among the flowing traffic and was soon lost in the maze of cars.

The second taxi had by now gone ahead of the first. They had to wait for the taxi carrying Ndumbe. The driver switched on the trafficator and signalled that he wanted to stop on the right hand side of the road. The man in the dark glasses and peak cap quickly disembarked. He stood by the car and surveyed the oncoming traffic. There it was. There was no mistake about it. There was the little Michelin sticker on the windscreen. He got into the taxi and ordered the driver to edge his way into the traffic. He succeeded in joining the traffic lane just as the taxi they were trailing went by. 'That's it, man, your driving is perfect,' he congratulated the driver. 'It's time we increased your bonus, don't you think so, boys?' The others agreed patting the driver on the back. 'Now concentrate all your attention on that taxi. We can't let go six million francs, just like that, eh, boys! That'll keep us going for sometime – the last haul was pretty small.'

Before they got to the Kawa Palace junction the traffic police officer turned and gave the oncoming traffic the right of way. The trafficators of Ndumbe's taxi winked, indicating that they wanted to stop in front of the hotel. The second taxi followed. Ndumbe alighted, paid the driver and walked into the hotel. He chose a small table laid for two, facing the main entrance into the dining hall.

A steward walked up to his table. 'Gin, Tonic,' he said simply. 'Gin, Tonic,' the steward repeated with a smile. 'English people drink Gin, Tonic. You Anglophone – Victoria, Buea, Kumba, Mamfe, Bamenda.' Ndumbe looked at him coldly and said nothing. The steward turned away. 'Gin, tonic for the mister,' he called out to the barman. 'Okay Gin, Tonic and bitters on rocks for the mister. Welcome, mister,' the barman repeated, picking up the bottle of gin from the shelf. He wiped the glass diligently with a napkin, measured two 'tots' into it and placed the bottle of tonic and bitters on the tray before him. The steward picked up the tray, walked to Ndumbe's table and served him. He sipped his drink as he glanced through the menu list. There was a wide choice. He wanted a quick lunch so as to get to Victoria before it was five o'clock. He was hungry and his immediate choice was 'Steak au Poivre'. At Kawa they gave you a really large chunk of juicy steak. That's why he liked the place – the thought of it always made his mouth water!

As he settled down to the first course – *crudités,* the swing doors opened and a gentleman in dark glasses and peak-cap came in and walked straight to his table. 'You don't mind if I join you?' 'Not at all,' Ndumbe replied instinctively without looking up. 'You are Mr. Ndumbe of Bobbie Customs Clearing Agency, Victoria? Pleased to meet you.' He put out his hand. Ndumbe looked up from his plate in surprise, put down his knife and took the hand. 'I don't think we've met before, have we? Please do sit down,' Ndumbe waved and pointed to the chair opposite him. 'Thanks,' the other man replied and sat down.

'Excuse me for butting in on you like this,' the man apologised profusely. 'I am doing a little business, you know . . . Import, Export. This is my business card.' He placed the card on the table. 'I understand reliably,' he went on, 'that you can be of great assistance in that regard.' He waited for

45

an answer. 'Yes that's so,' Ndumbe replied, raising his eyes from the plate. He did not like the camouflage and the man sitting opposite seemed to have sensed it. 'I understand . . . yes, I do . . . a question of identity. It was an accident. I was quite young when it happened – I lost my left eye. See . . . I've had to wear these dark glasses as a matter of necessity.' He added sadly, 'I look an awful sight without them.' Ndumbe felt so sorry for him. 'What a pity . . . how unfortunate,' Ndumbe exclaimed, a sad look on his face.

They ate their meal in silence, the man working on his strategy. He was not going to let six million francs slip through his fingers. 'You are going back to Victoria today?' It was the stranger who broke the silence. 'Of course, I shall, immediately after lunch,' Ndumbe confirmed looking at his watch.

'Well, I must be going. I am already late for some business appointment.' The man rose to go. 'It's been nice making your acquaintance. I hope this first contact will be to our mutual advantage – the prosperity of our two businesses.' 'Of course, yes . . . it's been a great pleasure meeting you,' Ndumbe cut in. 'Please don't hesitate to call on me when you are in Victoria. This is my card.' He handed over his card. The man looked at it for some time and nodded. 'Bobbie Customs Clearing Agency.' He repeated the words with some emphasis. They shook hands. The man walked through the swing doors, leaving his peak-cap on the table. He disappeared before the steward brought his bill. He had taken the meal on the house. That is what he told his friends who were still waiting in the car.

When Ndumbe left the hotel, he had decided he would go straight on to Victoria. As he came out of the hotel he was besieged by three taxi drivers, each trying to impress him with a good bargain. He brushed them aside, walked a little distance from the hotel and hailed a taxi, 'Motor Park?' 'Yes, patron – 200 francs.' When he arrived at the Motor Park, he decided he would hire a taxi. He would be the lone passenger. He found 'SAFE JOURNEY'. He knew the driver very well and they soon struck a bargain.

Ndumbe breathed a sigh of relief as he took his seat at the

back of the car, placing the brief case on his lap. Three other passengers accosted 'SAFE JOURNEY' as they were about to start off. 'Victoria . . . Victoria, trois places.' 'Sorry, I am on hire,' the driver replied and turned the car towards the Wouri Bridge. The three passengers quickly joined their own taxi and followed. The first taxi went through the old trunk road through Bonaberi. The second taxi followed. Ndumbe's taxi stopped at one of the local bakeries where the driver bought five loaves of bread. They later joined the main road again and headed for Victoria. The taxi carrying the four men followed.

At the junction where the road forked in the direction of Tiko and Nkongsamba, Ndumbe felt 'pressed' and told the driver to stop so that he could relieve himself. The other taxi overtook them and continued in the direction of Tiko. When Ndumbe continued his journey again they found the other taxi parked further up the road side. All the occupants remained in the car and as soon as Ndumbe's taxi overtook them, they followed.

There was something curious about one of the occupants of the taxi. Ndumbe thought he recognised the man in the dark glasses. Could it be the same man with whom he had dined earlier? What could he be doing here? He had not said he was travelling to Victoria! Were they being trailed? What a silly thought – it seemed so ridiculous! He dismissed it and he and the driver discussed the wave of murders by head hunters in Douala. They concluded it was a matter for the police and left it at that.

The first taxi had come on a straight stretch of road, just after Bekoko. He gave the clearance sign and signalled to the trailing taxi to overtake. It did not. The driver looked into his mirror. The taxi was only a few yards behind them. He signalled again. The taxi made no progress. 'This is curious,' he thought. He changed into a low gear, accelerated, gained some speed and slipped in the speed gear. The car shot like a bullet and sped away. He managed to put in some distance between them, but the trailing taxi had also picked up speed and continued to follow them.

The driver was not sure whether he was being followed so

47

he decided to stop again. The trailing taxi overtook them, went on until it was completely out of their view. 'Is there anything wrong?' Ndumbe asked the driver. 'Patron, I am trying to find out something. I am not sure, but I think we are being followed by the group of four in that taxi that overtook us a while ago.' 'What makes you think so,' Ndumbe asked simply with no concern in his voice. And even as they discussed the possibilities, they could see a car parked about half a kilometre ahead of them. As they drew near, it appeared that the car had had a breakdown. The driver was bending over the opened bonnet. The three others were waving frantically for them to stop. This time Ndumbe was certain he recognised the man in the dark glasses and immediately grew suspicious. 'Don't stop,' he ordered. The car sped on, the needle clocking the 120 kilometre limit.

The breakdown hoax by the group of four had not worked. So they clambered again into their taxi and pursued. 'I am now convinced that that vehicle behind is trailing us,' the driver said to Ndumbe. He told the driver to turn left in the direction of Tiko Town through Street Five on to the road leading to the District Office. 'Then turn left and we shall get on again to the main road out of Tiko and head for Victoria,' Ndumbe ordered. The driver obeyed. It took just fifteen minutes to do the detour.

There was no sign of the trailing taxi from the Likomba junction through Mutengene. On arrival at Mile Four the driver picked up the trailing taxi again in his mirror. This time it 'zoomed' past at very great speed. It was the last they saw of the taxi.

Ndumbe arrived in Victoria at 5 o'clock, just in time to attend an Executive Meeting of the Sasse Old Boys' Association (SOBA) at the Victoria Club. It was a brief meeting intended to put some finishing touches to the arrangements in connection with their yearly get together scheduled for Saturday, 21st November.

After the meeting, he offered a round of drinks and excused himself. He thought of the six million francs he was still carrying around in the brief case and decided he'd better get home before it was dark.

He left the Club, turned right and walked up towards the Clerks' Quarters. Then he took the short cut which passes by the Posts and Telecommunications Automatic Exchange on the left. Halfway through, some thirty metres from 'Buckingham Palace', three men appeared suddenly and attacked him. Before he could recover from the surprise they hit him in the face and in a flash the brief case had gone! 'My money, my money,' he shouted as he lashed at the last man and before he too got away he had sustained a deep cut just above the right eye. A large and sympathetic crowd soon gathered as news of the incident went round, six million francs! They could not believe it. Why should he be carrying around six million francs in a brief case!

'Help me ... help me ... the thieves may at this very moment be leaving for Douala. They trailed me all the way from Douala. Here is the number of the taxi they were travelling in. Yes ... in a Renault 12. Yes ... that's it. Please help me ... Help me for God's sake,' he pleaded. He was now behaving like a mad man!

A strategy was planned there and then. One group of volunteers was to keep watch at the Victoria Motor Park. The second was to search for a Douala-based taxi with the registration number given by Ndumbe. The third was to comb all the drinking houses in the vicinity. The clues – one man, tall and stocky, wearing dark glasses and a peak-cap; the second with a fresh cut above the right eye; a dirty brown brief case (Samsonite, made in Belgium, no keys, opened by secret code numbers). That was all. The groups dispersed.

After only fifteen minutes, the taxi was spotted. It was parked some distance away from the Presbyterian Youth Centre. There was no one in it. They decided on what to do. They deflated all the tyres and waited in the background. The group keeping watch at the Motor Park had also done a bit of on-the-spot investigation. Members of the Motor Transport Syndicate were prepared to cooperate. They too were watching for any strange and suspicious characters. The third group did not have to go far. There were a lot of men and women seated and drinking in the first licensed premises they entered. It was agreed that only one of them should go in.

The rest were to wait within observation range of the main exits.

Mark quickly surveyed the scene before him. It was too early in the evening and there were only a few customers at the time. His attention was attracted by a burly fellow sitting alone on the further side. The man was wearing dark glasses and a peak-cap. Mark pretended he was going to the toilets and took a good look at him from close range. This man fitted the description they had been given. And there it was – the dirty brown brief case! The man had it between his legs. This must be the man they were looking for. Satisfied, he went out to alert the rest. As he walked back into the bar, the man rose from the table brief-case in hand and strode across towards the exit. Mark at once interrupted him and seized the brief case. This lightning move took the man completely by surprise and before he collected his wits, Mark stretched out his palm gave him a violent 'chop' just below the gullet and followed it with a hard punch in the stomach. The man was strong and tried to fight back. The rest of the group closed in on him and mob justice took over. They hit him right and left – the type of thing a boxer does to a punchbag. By the time Mark realised that the man was in real danger and shouted – 'Hold it Boys' he had been kicked and trampled upon a dozen times. He was just a mass of crumpled shivering flesh. He was bleeding from the nose, ears and mouth. 'Serves him right . . . Serves him right,' was all the assembled crowd yelled.

Mark still clutched the brief case. He examined it. There were no signs that it had been tampeted with. Ndumbe who was later led to the scene identified it. Tears of joy coursed down his face as he feverishly tried to compose the code numbers. The brief case opened and there were his six million francs, safe and untouched!

While arrangements were being made to get the police on the scene, the other three members of the group had found their way to their taxi. The waiting group of volunteers allowed them to get into the car before they converged on them.

No questions were asked. They pulled them forcibly out of the car and the spontaneity and fury of mob justice once more came into play. A jeering crowd soon assembled to watch the spectacle. They spat on the three men, jostled them, beat them, stoned and kicked until they collapsed. 'Let's get some petrol and set up a human pyre, like they do in Lagos,' someone shouted. 'Yes . . . yes . . . good idea. Serves them right . . . Serves them right,' the crowd continued to yell. But the petrol had not arrived when the siren of the police car wailed in the distance.

No one in that crowd was prepared to give any evidence. The crowd dispersed within minutes.

The police found three battered men. They knew what had happened. They examined them. Their chests still heaved. They conferred for a while and decided the three were hospital cases. They were taken to hospital.

No Escape

'We are going to teach these bastards a lesson. A lesson they will never forget; that will go down in history. For all our endeavours and sacrifices over the years to bring this country to its present state of development, we will not stomach any more insults from undeserving, wanton and ungrateful idiots. I count on you all to execute this sacred mission. And remember it is now or never.'

The speaker paused thoughtfully. He surveyed the small group of soldiers whose assignment it was to seal off a section of the capital city of Yaounde and prevent possible movements of contending troops and reinforcements.

'Any questions?' There was a silence – an uneasy calm. Then one of them ventured: 'This is a rebellion, isn't it, Captain?' The other thought for a moment before he replied. 'Er-r-r, No. Not exactly. It is called a coup d'état, you don't only rebel but you also seize power.'

'And if we fail . . . I mean the consequences.' The Captain frowned. 'Don't ask such silly questions,' he blurted harshly. 'We are an army of liberation, destined to win. And who said soldiers make such mistakes; what do you think we learn strategy for; bloody fools we should call ourselves if we fail! In any case, civilians have never been known to hold out against the military.' His tone was agitated and sarcastic.

Having concluded, he stared with fierce concentration at the questioner.

That settled it. The rest of his listeners looked at each other and nodded in agreement. The embarrassed questioner was for some moments lost in thought.

So this was the beginning of disunity and instability! His country had known peace since the early turbulent years immediately after independence, although surrounded by neighbours who had tasted the effects and aftermath brought about by the inordinate ambitions of their own citizens; for him, this was a completely new trend in the country's politics!

He was not fighting for a cause – certainly not in defence of the motherland!

He had a young wife and two children. And an old mother. What would happen to them if he got killed? The idea of the triumphal entry into heaven did not impress him; neither did the amulet he wore under his shirt containing a parchment of the 'holy book,' believed to neutralise the deadly shock of bullets.

Then suddenly certain lines in the second verse of the National Anthem struck him forcibly. He recited them in silent prayer:

> Muster thy sons in close union around thee
> Mighty as the Buea Mountain be their team
> Instil in them the love of gentle ways
> Regret for errors of the past
> Foster for mother Africa (Cameroon) a loyalty
> That true shall remain to the last.

He did not recite the refrain but ended with a sigh. He had realised it was now too late; the explosion was inevitable.

Captain Dewa was content within himself, stimulated by his mission, the excitement, the belief of the rightness of it all, the promise of it all, and the hopes, BIG HOPES. At thirty, he had been tipped as the likely military Governor of the South West Province after the successful overthrow of the civilian Government. If he had a choice of residence on taking command, he would prefer the 'Schloss' – the celebrated German Governor's residence in Buea. The civilian Government's idea of designating it a public monument, he thought stupid and wasteful.

Dewa was not a particularly bright student while training at the Armed Forces Training Centre at Ngaundere (CIFAN), the Training and Proficiency Centre at Ngaoundal (CEFAN), the Specialist Centre in Yaounde (CISA) and the Military Academy, Yaounde (EMIA). His progress had been rapid and over that of his better qualified colleagues who were destined to climb their 'tree' the hard way owing to a policy of *avancement aux choix*. Qualifications meant nothing; talent meant nothing; merit meant nothing!

The previous evening he had been summoned to a meeting of the presidential guard top-brass for the final briefing, and the delegation of specific powers after the coup. The scheme of manoeuvres, the movement and storming action of the troops on the strategic and sensitive establishments; those to be taken as hostages, communication between the 'attacking forces' by walkie-talkie on a secret frequency – all these were discussed in detail. It was revealed that special combat uniforms for the mission were not ready. This had been due to a re-scheduling of D–day as a result of certain government measures which included the deployment of members of the presidential guard. It had been decided to wear red armbands for identification purposes.

Two lists had been prepared: The Black List which contained those who were thought potentially dangerous. These would be eliminated or detained immediately. The White List, of those who might be counted upon to cooperate and help.

The possible reaction of the civilian population – favourable or otherwise – was then discussed; they had to count on their support! It was argued that a swift but smooth takeover would certainly shock the civilian population into complete acceptance of a situation brought about by what they called the 'recklessness and planlessness of the civilian regime'. If the capital territory fell, it would be easy to woo the numerous 'chorus groups' to send the first messages of support and solidarity. The ensuing 'avalanche' from the rest of the regions would crown it all. That was the consensus.

The national radio network came in here for mention. It must be taken over and guarded at all costs. For the effective coverage and dissemination of information and proclamations, it was imperative that the residences of all senior technical and news staff of the radio be located and put under round-the-clock surveillance. The public relations committee was to see to that.

Then the conduct of the rebellion was agreed upon: No indiscriminate killings; contending forces must be ruthlessly crushed; take no prisoners; shoot all deserters and looters; no harrassment of the civilian population; minimum destruction of the infrastructure; password – OPERATION HYENA.

The logistics expert and strategist, an expatriate technical adviser, was congratulated for the brief and comprehensive report presented. It showed that the military hardware in their possession greatly outweighed that of the government forces both in quantity and sophistication. These included French, Belgian, Russian and Israeli made automatic firearms. His intelligence machinery reported that, so far, the coup plot had remained a secret thus maintaining that important element of surprise in military tactics – catching the enemy with their pants down. He predicted that barring any unforeseen circumstance, Yaounde would fall in a matter of hours.

The assembly then moved into the Operations Centre. In the middle was a giant map of Yaounde and its environs. There were areas shaded in green and red with arrows and coloured flagged pins indicating the movements and the tactical positioning of the storming troops led by mechanised units including armoured vehicles into blocking positions. Here the expert pounded home the operation objectives.

Other plans included the jamming of the military communications system to prevent any contact with regional commands, the severing of telephone links and the taking over of power and water installations.

The text of the proclamation presented at the meeting was considered verbose, uninspiring and not reflecting the spirit and the revolution. It had, for instance, omitted the suspension of the constitution and its institutions, the respect by the new regime of the obligations and commitments of the deposed regime, and a warning to Foreign diplomatic missions to restrain from any action that tended to undermine the sovereignty and territorial integrity of the nation. The guidelines for the final text were given and a drafting committee of three, one senior military official and two top civil servants, was charged with its redrafting.

The meeting came to a conclusion. The leader of the group assured his listeners of complete victory over what he called 'forces of disunity'. The hard part, he said, was to gain the position of authority, and once that was attained the rest would be easy. 'The more power you have the easier it is to find solutions to any problems. You merely surround yourself with the right people, the right brains – they come up with the answers and the solutions. The credit and glory will be ours.' That sounded quite sensible! They clapped enthusiastically. There was a lot of back-slapping as the leader moved round, chatting freely with everyone.

Dewa was meeting the commander-in-chief for the first time. He stood a good six foot plus. He had a substantial physique but his voice was too mellow for a senior military officer.

Dewa stood stiffly at attention throughout their brief encounter. He finally shook his hand with a graceful bow of the head, his left hand behind his back. Here he was among the trusted ones – one of those to rule and direct the affairs of the nation after the takeover! His trend of thought was interrupted by the thud of clicking-boots. All came to attention as the commander-in-chief left the hall, his right hand raised high up above his head in the 'thumbs-up' signal. They all raised their hands in unison, and saluted as the jeep departed.

The tense and hushed atmosphere in the room now gave place to light-hearted banter.

The time was 2.30 a.m. thirty tense and anxious minutes to ZERO HOUR. Dewa himself took the roll-call. There were fifty soldiers under his command. They all sat restless as he paced the corridor, giving last minute instructions. A couple of them were already experiencing the effects of the combat 'shots' and were keyed up for the battle.

Earlier he had carried out a kit inspection, insisting that iron rations must be carried; he thought they might come in handy.

The minutes and seconds ticked away. Transport vehicles had lined up with troops at the ready, their engines running as they awaited the orders to strike. Then a tense voice crackled over the rebel communication system. 'This is OPERATION HYENA Operation Headquarters OB calling.

Are you receiving me? Come in LION, over.' 'Receiving you clean and clear, Sir, over.' 'Come in SCORPION, over.' 'Ever ready Sir, over.' 'Come in TORTOISE over.' 'Receiving you Sir, over.' The final instructions then followed.

'This is operation headquarters, OBILI, calling all loyal units. This is the start of the people's revolution. Remember it is now or never. I count on your support and loyalty. Good luck to you all.'

The revolution had begun. The Hyena Lion commanded by Dewa had taken the strategic positions at the city's centre, blocking all the main access roads with barbed wire entanglements. The road blocks were each manned, visibly, by two soldiers armed with sub-machine guns, while about ten others stayed in the background, completely out of view.

Although explosions and periodical short bursts of gun fire were heard all over Yaounde, most inhabitants did not learn what had happened until late afternoon the following day. The troop movements had been mistaken for military training exercises.

The progress of the fighting was being monitored and co-ordinated from field operation reports communicated by units. Operations Centre reported the taking over of the national radio, the airport, power and water installations. There had been no resistance. The proclamation had been broadcast nationwide and relative calm had been reported. Stiff resistance in the siege of the presidential palace was reported in morale-boosting language.

Captain Dewa relayed the good news to his comrades. There were hopes, big hopes for those who would live after the takeover.

The battle situation remained relatively the same until the airforce helicopters and transport planes took to the skies. As Dewa's group decided to take cover, one of the helicopters roared low over the Obili Barracks. There were loud explosions. All attempts by Captain Dewa to contact operations headquarters after the attack had failed – the secret radio communications system had been silenced.

'This is a very serious situation,' Dewa told his comrades. 'I cannot now contact headquarters. I don't know what's

happening.' No one replied but he sensed a tinge of desperation on their faces. He thought this unsoldierly behaviour for
'heroes' – the elite arm of the regular forces.

Minutes later, a member of his group disappeared. Dewa
knew he would not have gone far. He moved stealthily,
straining his ears for any sounds. Suddenly a bareheaded
figure in battle-dress and unarmed emerged about thirty
yards away. He wore no red armband. This was the deserter.
He raised his rifle. The conduct of the rebellion permitted
this. He pulled the trigger. There was only a muffled scream
as the escaping soldier threw up his arms and fell on his back
– a shuddering mass of flesh. A *coup de grâce* was not
necessary. The sprawling corpse was left where it had fallen.

The explosions from the direction of the Obili Barracks
continued and now and then the noise of steady small-arms
gun fire came closer. Two armoured cars rumbled in their
direction bristling with machine guns. The rebels made a
courageous attempt to stop them. They succeeded in dis-
abling one of them by shooting at the tyres. Although it
finally came to a halt, its guns blazed away in all directions
taking a considerable toll of lives. The other continued,
smashing its way through the road blocks with ease.

Captain Dewa knew the end of the rebellion had come.
Here he was surrounded by the dead, the dying and the
wounded. He moved forward trying to ignore their moans
and feeble cries for help. He felt a hand weakly grasp his
trousers but fell away at the next step. He told himself, he
must not stop for anything or anybody. He had to escape. He
started weeping for his mother, wife and child. He wondered
what would be said later about him. A deserter, killed in
action or reported missing? He knew what would happen to
him if he was caught – face a charge of high treason, felony
and murder and finally the firing squad. He thought of
giving himself up. A good soldier never surrendered; too
cowardly, he told himself.

He thought of Mariatu, his girlfriend, living at Briquterie.
He could take refuge there? No, he told himself again and
again. They were likely to search for him there.

The Operation HYENA had gone awry. It was a fiasco.

Logistically it had appeared a relatively simple operation. A quick mop-up victory had now escalated into a much more complicated affair. The mistake had been the underestimation of the foe. The fight to martyrdom was lost.

The only option now was escape. But through what route? The following were open to him: southwards through Mbalmayo, Sangmelima on to Bertoua, Batouri, Yokadouma, Molundu into the Central African Republic. The second through Ebolowa, Kribi and Campo into Equatorial Guinea. The third by train to Douala, Tiko, Limbe, by boat to Oron in Nigeria. The fourth was through Bafia, Bafoussam, Dschang through Mbo country into Mamfe, then on to Ekok and Abakaliki in Nigeria.

The first three routes he considered unsafe. He knew there would be a round the clock vigil at all the main routes out of Yaounde for escaping rebels. He preferred the Yaounde–Bafoussam route through Mbo country along bush-paths to Mamfe. He judged that in the Western Region where the inhabitants had lived through a turbulent post independence era, people would normally prefer to go about their lawful business of harvesting and planting coffee than bother themselves with the antics of government. To them nothing else would matter as long as they sold their coffee. He was sure they did not even know that a rebellion was taking place!

Dewa's first problem was how to obtain some clothes. He had remained in hiding in a sparsely built-up area dominated by government offices, around the municipal lake. He had earlier watched a man hanging clothes on a line to dry. These included a pair of blue jeans and a Bastos 'T' shirt. As soon as it was getting dark he came out of hiding and stole the clothes. The jeans fitted nicely. Soon he had discarded his camouflage uniform and all except a sum of five hundred thousand francs, the initial sum he had been paid the day before, for his participation in the rebellion. He finally dumped his German-made HK21 rifle into the lake and walked on to the road.

There were not many people about and he gathered from scraps of conversation that fighting was still going on. His heart thumped with great excitement. There were hopes that he could make the trip by road via Bafia before the security forces spread their drag-net.

He took the first lorry he found bound for Bafoussam carrying a cargo of cement. The journey was long, bumpy and uneventful; he had slept for most of the time. Bafoussam was quiet – 'asleep' – except for one or two late taxis which honked time and again for no apparent reason, and the distant noise of blaring loudspeakers playing Makossa music.

He was not hungry. The iron rations had sustained him for nearly twenty-four hours. He had to get out of Bafoussam before dawn to avoid being caught in a security check; he had no identification papers. As he walked quickly along the road he came on a drove of cattle being herded for the long trek. What luck, he thought. He could join the drovers disguised as one of them! That was it. He soon found the three and spoke in the language they understood. They listened to his story; apparently they had heard nothing about the rebellion.

They provided him with a white flowing robe and a skull-cap to match, a spear and a sheathed dagger. They then shaved his thick hair down to the skin of his skull. The disguise was perfect. They told him the trail was long. He said he did not mind. He had been accustomed to road-treks during his training.

They were out of Bafoussam just as the first rays of the sun peeped from the east. They entered the trail along little hamlets and villages and left the hustle and bustle of the town behind. They halted to say their prayers while the cows moved freely cropping the green wet grass.

The first night Dewa's mind went through the events of the past few days. That bloody traitor of a logistic expert had failed them. He had messed things up. But all along he'd been so optimistic about it all! Now the military governor designate of the South West Province was on the run – a fugitive! He hoped he would make the Nigerian border and declare himself a political refugee under the United Nations Human Rights Declaration. He felt completely exhausted both mentally and physically, his nerves almost numb by the haunting horrors Operation HYENA had held. The moans and cries of the maimed and dying, the din of sporadic gun fire,   even   the overwhelming smell of bloating corpses. He was now far away from the scene. He slept as he had never slept before.

For five days they trekked over predominantly grasslands at an altitude that made trekking less exhausting with little or no menace from the tse-tse fly. From Dschang they went over the Mbo Plains into Fontem, Atebong, Tali and Bakebe into Mamfe. Here, news of the abortive coup was discussed everywhere, bluntly and freely. He heard ridiculous accounts and rumours about everything, including an impending invasion by Libyan and Moroccan mercenaries. There was outright condemnation of the 'plotters and enemies of peace'. There were calls for more vigilance and maximum punishment for those who they said had introduced 'gangster politics'. He was disappointed by those who said a military regime would not have done any better! Throughout the trek he had remained in the background while the hanggling with the dealers and butchers went on.

They found a long queue of transport vehicles. Armed security officials swarmed all over the place, like hornets, interrogating and demanding identity papers from nervous passengers. A few of them had left their papers at home. That was no excuse, they were told. They were detained for further questioning.

The cows and their four drovers continued their long trek past the check-point. They all looked so innocent – ordinary Cameroonians going about their lowly occupation. 'Get moving, you there,' one of the soldiers ordered, waving his hand. The cows and the men continued their journey towards the Nigerian border. Dewa felt the cold sweat on his brow and neck. What luck! What a relief! 130 kilometres and he would be out of Cameroon and on to FREEDOM! They looked at each other. No one spoke.

They stopped about two miles away from the check-point. They said their prayers. Dewa prayed for himself and the family he had left behind.

He had fallen asleep soon after, quite oblivious of everything else around him. Then he dreamt he'd been making love to Mariatu and woke up suddenly, feeling quite spent and an ugly sticky wetness around his loins.

Now, where was he? He looked around, giving his eyes a good rub. He soon realised he was in strange surroundings. Then his mind became alert; he was now alone! What had happened to the cows and his kinsmen? They had thought it best to abandon and desert him!

A wave of hot anger swept through him. Then he shook with rage. 'The damned, bloody bastards,' he fumed. He wished he were armed; that would have settled it; shot them in the back. He gathered himself and picked up the trail.

Dewa had calmed down by the time he caught up with them. They only nodded a welcome and one of them explained that they did not wish to disturb his deep slumber. He did not reply. He was a rebel run-away soldier, and should do nothing that would erode his chances of escape. He thought of paying them some 'hush' money but he had finally suppressed the urge to do so. His life could be in great danger if they discovered he had money on him.

They had arrived at the border-town of Ekok, where there had been a lull in business activities; the Nigerian Military Government had ordered the closure of their borders in their historic operation – *New Naira for old*. Security officials swarmed everywhere like locusts. They searched, interrogated, checked identification papers and even scrutinised faces. In the mean time, the identities of the coup leaders had been established and were rightly classified as 'wanted persons'. A nation-wide man-hunt, compared only to the pre-and post-independence era of the *Maquisard*, had commenced. There were long queues of vehicles and persons waiting to take their turns before the screening panels at road-blocks and check-points.

Dewa's three companions had checked-out, but he was asked to wait with the rest who had no identification papers. They were 'herded' to an area and closely watched by armed soldiers.

He did not panic like most of them. His 'particulars' had been lost. He thought over it again. 'Lost' would give the impression of carelessness on his part. No. That would not do. 'Stolen', he thought. Yes, that was the right word. He would say he had reported the loss to the police, who had advised him to renew them as soon as possible. As soon as possible also meant at the earliest opportunity! The opportunity had not presented itself! That was his defence. There was nothing to fear! He still had good cover. He looked like an ordinary herdsman – hair shaved down to the skull, filthy-looking boubou with skull-cap to match, prayer kettle and beads, a bow and quiver full of poison-tipped arrows and a six-inch dagger. He was convinced the disguise would go by.

'Now, get a move on and see about the fellows without papers,' the officer said to his second-in-command. Then he announced without any fuss for all to hear. 'We are sorry for the inconvenience, but the now uncertain situation of the country warrants the measures being taken to safeguard life and property, and in the overall interest of the nation. You all know, as well as I do, that every Cameroonian *must* carry a National Identity Card on his person; too bad if you left it at home.'

A long ripple of suppressed tittle-tattle, passed through the little crowd. The majority of them were harmless, ordinary peasants, who only remembered to carry their papers when they travelled to the city. Others, the petty-traders, whose love for making money transcended other considerations including civic obligations, were ready to bribe their way through.

Dewa had taken the hint given earlier in the warning by the officer-in-charge of the operation. He edged his way through from the top of the queue. How would he explain his being in possession of five hundred thousand francs? He thought of handing over the money to one of the traders for safe-keeping; but how could he do this with everyone watching? and what would happen if the trader disappeared with the money? No. He was not prepared to take the risk. But he was a herdsman who sold cows as he travelled from one place to the other. Was he also not a trader?

He tried to absolve himself of total blame. He told the soldier that his papers had been stolen; he intended to renew them as soon as possible.

'You talking bull-shit. What you mean "as soon as possible"; as soon as possible means what? Do you think I'm here to listen to that shit . . .? Next.'

Dewa moved on. There were two other soldiers, a captain and a second-lieutenant sitting side by side. The one with the sun-shades seemed to fix his gaze on Dewa as he walked over and sat down in front of them. The other fired him with questions – when and where he was born, the names of his parents, where he went to school, etc. The other in the glasses just sat there, his arms folded across his chest, saying nothing, just looking, looking and looking. Dewa could feel his eyes boring right through him.

Why didn't he say something? Why wouldn't he take off those damn glasses so he could guess what was on his mind? And what the hell was he after?

The two conferred briefly. Then the one in the glasses stood up and asked Dewa to follow. He followed and acted as ordered. He unshouldered the quiver and emptied it. There were ten iron-tipped arrows. 'They are all poisoned, you know,' he warned, as he put them back carefully, one by one, not touching the tips. The other did not reply. He ordered Dewa to raise his hands. He then frisked him expertly. But that was a stupid order – raise your hands. Who told the bastard he was prepared to surrender! He found the dagger. Then he felt his hands moving deftly up his right thigh. They stopped; an object strapped there! 'Well, let's see what's here . . . if it's marijuana, then you're in for something really bad.' The soldier unwrapped the little bundle and found the money. Dewa would have liked to watch the expression on his face; he still had his glasses on.

'The spoils of war,' he muttered as he put the money away into his pocket. Perhaps they would set him free! Let him get on to safety through the border. That was his prayer; and hadn't they just taken ransom money?

The interrogation commenced once more. There was no mention of the money recovered from him. The soldier in the dark glasses said nothing; he just sat looking, looking and looking straight at him. The questioner had changed his tactics. He was now being buffetted and badgered incessantly with questions. 'I put it to you . . . I put it to you that . . .'

They finally took him to another room. There were three

others seated as he walked in. They all stood up and saluted. Then the senior of the three addressed him. 'Captain Dewa, in the name of the President of the Republic, I am taking you into lawful custody.' The lieutenant in the dark glasses walked in with the hand-cuffs. He took off the glasses just before he clicked the hand-cuffs shut. 'Mon capitaine,' he said sadly, 'Vous êtes dans le foyer de trahison . . . c'ést domage, mon capitaine.'

Dewa recognised him. He was the little truant who spent some time in his unit. That was a long time ago, he remembered. He simply nodded recognition.

Dewa realised the game was up. There on the wall were blown-up photographs of his other colleagues who headed the rebellion. There was now no escape. How he wished he had died in the heat of the battle, fighting for the cause. Yes, he thought; to take his rightful place among the *faithful*.

The Square Peg

The man walked from the Moliwe Workers' Village to the old Ombe Bridge, built in 1919, a distance of four kilometres to commit suicide. When he arrived at the bridge, he stood gazing hesitantly at the tumbling waters fourty metres below. What he saw in the depths sent a shiver down his spine. He was afraid to die.

Memba (alias Fineboy) was unemployed. He was not what one would call a lazy man. He was healthy and of good physique. But he was the rolling-stone-type; the square peg that always found itself in the round hole; the jack of all trades, who was evidently master of none. His colleagues were getting on well in life, but he had been a failure – a disgrace to his family, and to manhood.

In his thirty-sixth year, he had been a teacher, court-clerk, banana planter, trader and smuggler. These years had been a most trying time for him. As a teacher, he had been guilty of what the Ministry of Education termed 'gross misdemeanour.' He had seduced a female pupil and had his name struck off the register of teachers. As a customary court clerk, he had served a three year sentence with hard labour at the Buea Convict Prison. He had accepted a bribe. As a trader, he had been duped by his business partner and lost a fortune. He had also tried his hand at banana planting under a Small Holders Scheme run by the Extension Service of the Ministry of Agriculture. But the first severe tornado had blown down almost all the banana stems and ruined what would otherwise have been a rich harvest.

He had even tried smuggling. It had been a risky and tricky business. He had made a lot of money during the peak seasons through this illicit traffic of contraband goods across the border. All had gone well until the confrontation with members of his group and the frontier custom guards in a fierce gun-battle which left one officer and three of his comrades dead. He'd had a clean-shave having sustained only slight injuries; and he had vowed to give up smuggling.

Lastly, he had tried the army as a last resort. The Second World War was on and volunteers were being recruited, and so, a few weeks later, Memba was among fifty other Cameroonians who queued outside the Recruitment Office for enlistment into the West African Frontier Force.

'Your name?' the recruitment officer with sun-burnt features inquired in a commanding voice.

'Fineboy,' he replied curtly, standing stiffly at attention. The officer gave him a quick look. It was clear that this prospective recruit was trying to impress him. He had seen many like him during his two years as recruiting officer.

'What do you mean by Fineboy? I want your proper name.' The officer growled irritatingly.

'Oh, yes . . . my proper name.' The man scratched his head looking a bit confused. 'Musa . . . Memba . . . Saar.'

'Home?' the officer continued, preening his moustache.

'Bamoum'

'Where is that?' the officer queried.

'French Cameroon,' Memba replied, stiffening. The officer looked up at him from his position at the desk, his beady eyes askew. His eyes returned to the card in front of him. He signed it.

'Sergeant!' A tall man in a red sash and deeply scarred cheeks appeared, puffed his chest, stood at attention and saluted, clicking his boots in the process.

'Take the recruit to Captain Jones,' the recruitment officer ordered with a wave of his hand.

'Yes, Saar. . . .' the sergeant's voice boomed. He saluted and marched off. Memba followed.

A few minutes later, they were standing before Captain Jones, the Company medical officer, a corpulent fellow aged about thirty, in white overalls.

The medical examination was rigorous, but Memba satisfied the medical standards for enlistment into the Army, with regard to height, chest measurement, weight and vision, and was passed as fit for active service. After all the other formalities, Memba was issued with uniform. He received bush shirts, khaki shorts, brown kilmanock cap, puttees, belt and boots. He was next taken to the company's barber who gave him the 'recruit's cut'. Using a razor, he removed all the hair down to the skin of his skull.

So this was it, he thought. He was pleased with himself. He was now on active service – a man to be dreaded and feared. He imagined himself frowning and striking fear at the Victoria Market Women and carrying away what he fancied. He knew that soldiers do this during war time and get away with it.

And so Memba began a new life in the soldiers' barracks, a life which he had, so far, only looked at from outside the barbed wire fencing that encircled the barracks, as he took the short-cut to New Town Market. For the next three months, he was to receive instruction and training with special emphasis on physical fitness, drill and games.

Memba woke up the next morning to the sound of the bugle. It was six o'clock in the morning. He found himself 'falling-in' with about forty others. They all jog-trotted a distance of eight kilometres – beyond Mile Four and back. He could feel his lungs exploding and he almost stopped. 'Get Movin . . .' the sergeant urged in his harsh commanding voice. 'Hai .. hai . . . hai . . . .' the booted foot-falls almost drowning his voice.

In the barracks that evening, he went to bed early. He was not feeling very well. He was all aches and pains. In civilian life, he had been content with a few keep-fit exercises. Now, it was completely different. This training taxed his physical strength to the utmost.

He had tried to avoid this part of his training by reporting at the medical centre. He always complained of dizziness and what he described simply as 'bottom belly'. It was the first time Captain Jones had heard of such an ailment. There were no symptoms. No such disease had been discovered by the Tropical School of Medicine, where he had spent two years and obtained a diploma. His case baffled the medical authorities, and many questions were asked. One of them was whether it was contagious and if so, Memba had to be isolated. That was what happened.

He had been taken immediately to the isolation ward which was about one hundred metres from the nearest building.

Two civilian medical officers had been summoned to consti-
tute a medical board of three. Three days of thorough and
meticulous examination including tests, yielded only negative
results. The board was unanimous in its findings. An interesting case of 'deliberate malingering'. The military authorities
took a very serious view of the matter. From then on, Memba
had no breathing space. He participated in all training
activities with no exception.

Now, Memba cared very little about details. It was no
wonder, therefore, that he always got into trouble with his
command. He was considered a stubborn recruit and rele-
gated to the *Awkward Squad*. He had on more than one
occasion hurried to the parade ground with his right foot in
the left boot and vice versa.

'Was matter wi you deh?' the illiterate drill sergeant
charged with the *Awkward Squad* bellowed. 'Atten......shon!'
the order came. There was a thundering of boots on the
brown sun-baked parade ground, raising clouds of dust. The
sergeant walked through the ranks slowly inspecting the
group. It was then that he observed Memba's clumsiness – the
attention-posture did not appear to him normal. He bent
down to find out why.

'What you mean, you recruit? Why you no fit dress fine . . .
eh? You beast of no nation.' The sergeant's voice was agitated.
This raised suppressed laughter from the rest of the squad.
On other occasions his puttees were not tightly wound round
his legs. During one long drill-session Memba had tripped
when they got into a tangle during parade. The confusion
sent two other soldiers as well as him sprawling on the ground
in full kit.

During another of those inspection parades, the R.S.M.
had come to watch their progress. 'Atten......shon!' came the
voice of the drill sergeant. The squad sprang to attention.
'R...r...r...Twar'. Memba's thoughts must have been miles
away from the parade ground. He turned to the left. There
came the noise of clashing steel as the bayonet of his own rifle
and that of the soldier to his right came into violent contact.

'Nkatawah. . . damn. . . Burobaka,' the sergeant cursed in
Hausa. He marched briskly towards Memba, a six-footer

with substantial physique. 'Buckle-up . . . savvy?' he scowled, jabbing at Memba's ribs with his pace-stick.

'Yezz . . . Sam . . .' Memba replied, straightening stiffly to attention. The sergeant returned to his commanding position.

'Tanda....Ezzz......Tand Easy!' The squad eased up. They either fumbled with their caps and belts or put in a joke or two before the next command.

'Atten......shon!' the order resumed. Memba looked round anxiously. The Regimental Sergeant Major in the red-sash had arrived for the routine inspection. The drill sergeant marched a few paces forward, stamped his feet and saluted. The R.S.M. returned the salute. They held a brief conversation and both marched in step as he inspected the squad. Suddenly, the R.S.M. halted. 'Look sergeant!' he turned, pointing at Memba who had been fidgetting and looking round, trying to watch him.

'Look to your front, Number Four. If you want to look Major, parade ground no be de place.' The sergeant was furious. They both had a little chat and the sergeant turned round facing the squad. 'Come forward, Number Four!' he ordered. Memba hesitated. 'Kai,' the sergeant swore. He was losing his temper. 'Are you a craze or a mad? Christ, Almighty! I says fall-out.. you dam shit!' Memba moved five paces forward towards the sergeant. He had miscalculated; he ought to have taken three. They almost came face to face. He realised this too late. 'Fuck off,' the sergeant spluttered. The rest of the squad could not suppress their shock – there was no such command order! The laughter that erupted was contagious – it bubbled through the rank and file. Memba quickly did a right-about-turn, took two paces forward, then another right-about-turn. 'Sorry, Sir,' Memba apologised with a salute. 'You beast of no nation,' he cursed. 'I tell Commander plenty time dat you no fit make good soja. Everytime he tell me try again . . . you try him again. I don tire for you. Now, up deh . . . quick marsh,' he pointed to the other end of the parade ground.

This is what was commonly known with the West African Frontier Force as *Gwara-Gwara*. In the Police Force, it was simply called *Fatigue*. It was some form of punishment for slight and serious misdemeanour and what was considered unsoldierly behaviour. Memba found himself marching and jog-trotting under the full heat of the sun in full combat kit on the sun-baked ground.

So was the soldier's life, a little short of what he had expected. It was rough, disciplined and all too exacting.

He was in good spirits as he strolled later that evening to New Town. He had decided to have some fun, after the humiliation he had been subjected to earlier on the parade ground. While in New Town, an incident took place which ultimately caused his imprisonment and expulsion from the army with ignominy. He had overtaken a Bassa-man carrying a six-gallon tin of *'Miyok'* (palm-wine). He had insisted, quite against the man's will, that he be allowed to taste the palm-wine. 'Nyandom, tis no get law,' he had argued, and that had settled it. But he drank three bottles in the process of tasting and had refused to pay. 'We deh go fight for Burma for you, eh . . . Mimbo-man . . . no talk dat foolish . . . make I pay for what?' The palm-wine seller's remark was equally sarcastic. He asked whether it was the uniform he was wearing that gave him the right to steal. In any case, he did not know where *'Burma'* was, and cared even less – war or no war.

A fight ensued during which a group of wine-sellers joined forces and had the soldier well-beaten. When the news reached the barracks, the soldiers came out in large numbers to avenge their colleague's fate. A free-for-all brawl followed; mimbo-man used his cutlass freely in self-defence, slashing away at any uniformed figure that came his way. Before the situation was brought under control, four soldiers and three civilians lay dead. Forty others were seriously injured.

After the judicial inquiry into the causes of the Palm-wine Riots or 'Mimbo-War', as the incident came to be known, Memba's comportment was described by the learned judge, President of the Commission, as the 'last straw that broke the camel's back'. He was convicted – imprisonment with hard labour – and dismissed from the army with ignominy.

Three years went by and Memba had served his full term. They were three hard years of suffering, deprivation and humiliation. He had been put with the 'night-soil' gang. Their daily routine was to empty human faeces into specially manufactured buckets. They carried their load through the streets to a dumping creek, away from the town. He remembered that passers-by used to avoid them, calling them 'shit-boys', covering their noses to keep away the smell.

Now, out of prison, he found himself broken down in spirit, health and with no means of livelihood. Life had treated him badly; life was not worth living anymore – not after all he had been through. Dead men faced no trials, sorrows or tribulations. In utter desperation, therefore, he had made up his mind to commit suicide.

Now, how would he take away his life? That was his immediate problem. He first thought of drinking a good quantity of some liquid detergent, locally known as 'camel-water' (also used by abortionists). He thought the matter over again and decided against it. You died a slow and painful death; many a time you were taken into hospital after you blacked-out and saved by some stroke of luck. A hit or miss affair.

Then he thought of hanging by the neck from a rope. That too was very painful. You started regretting you'd chosen to die that way, and as it often happens, there's no one around at the time to cut the rope!

Then another thought came to him – like a flash. The Ombe Bridge? Yes, that would do. He would throw himself down into the depths. He would be dizzy by the time he got to the bottom, hit the huge slimy boulders below, get smashed into a shuddering mound of flesh. Dead. Finished. Gone. Then the torrent will do the rest; flush the remains down, scattered into the seven seas; a much more respectable way to die. His mind was made up.

It was a thirty-minute walk from the Moliwe Camp. When he did arrive at the bridge, he stood contemplating on how he would fall – with his head first or just take a plunge. Then the thought came to him. He still had time for a little prayer. It was a short prayer – 'Lord, forgive me for what I'm going to do.' He signed himself. He took a last look from the bridge. The boulders jutted out here and there invitingly: he could hear the deafening roar of the cascading waters below.

Then his courage left him. He suddenly felt a pain in the head. His body grew limp as the feet gave way under him. 'Help me .. help me ...' he let out a frightened scream, clutched desperately at the iron railing, slid down slowly and collapsed on the bridge.

The Scrap Heap

The radio had announced the Administrative Dispositions over the National network at one o'clock. Martin's Number Two in the Ministry had been named his successor. Nothing had been said about him. He had neither been transferred nor re-assigned. He was simply dropped. He, too, had joined the never-ending queue of waiters. How long would he have to wait? Two years? Some had stayed on the scrap heap for more!

Martin deliberately refused to panic. But there were the immediate problems. Where would he live when he left the posh rent-free quarters? He knew he had to be quick before he was thrown out. He had started building a house in his home town but had not completed it. How long would he remain on the scrap heap? How would he live on his now drastically cut emoluments, shorn of multifarious allowances? 'I've had it,' he thought, as he switched off the radio and rose to fetch himself a drink.

There was still a bottle of champagne in the refrigerator. He tried to count the number of champagne bottles he had opened since he became Secretary General. This would be the last for some time, unless he was re-assigned to some other top post.

His thoughts wandered as he tried to open the bottle. Suddenly he felt the upward thrust from the cork. Before he recollected his straying thoughts, the cork flew off, hitting the ceiling above him with a bang, a fine foamy spray following in its wake. The champagne drenched his face and clothes. He looked at the bottle; half its contents had gone! 'Showers of blessing,' he thought, as he filled his glass.

He had just taken the first sip when the telephone rang. 'Condolences for losing my job,' he said to himself, as he lifted the receiver. It was his wife, telephoning from his home town. How relieved he felt as he spoke to her! They too had heard the announcement. 'But how could they do this to you?' she screamed. He could sense the tension in her voice. She told him members of the family had gathered to console her and that many of them were still there. She said she wanted to join him immediately to help ease the worry and anxiety that was now inevitable.

Martin had also spoken to his father-in-law. 'Take it like a man,' he had said. 'It is like going to war. Now, what do you expect? You are either shot and killed, maimed or you survive. That's just it. We could have been shamed if you took bribes or stole public money and went to prison. God forbid. This is only a temporary set-back, I tell you, and mark my words.'

When Martin hung up later, he felt better. A temporary set-back was what his father-in-law had called it. He hoped he was right. 'For me,' he told himself, 'the sky is the limit.'

Martin Ngombe was a highly placed civil servant with years of experience behind him, having been a civil servant during the colonial administration. He had gone through the mill to attain the enviable post of Permanent Secretary, in pursuance of a progressive policy of Africanisation. He was therefore what was commonly known as a 'top' civil servant. Post Independence, with the desire to catch up with the rest of the world, saw him at the top – Secretary General under the country's new civil service set-up.

Martin was a conscientious civil servant. He fitted into a group which newly independent countries preferred to call 'the professionally conscious'. He still referred to General Orders, when subordinate staff had to comply with matters of discipline and was generally thought to be too strict, too efficient, too meticulous and too officious – words which suggested he overdid things.

It was said that he had himself supervised the taking of an inventory at the official residence of a highly placed 'big-shot', shortly after the latter had been removed from office, on the suspicion that government property, including carpets, had been removed to his home town. The inventory indeed revealed a loss of government property for which the 'big-shot' was surcharged.

Many agreed that Martin was vigilant, doing his job without fear or favour, in keeping with the British tradition which was expressed simply, *politicians come and go, but the Civil Service remains*. Others said he had ridiculed the set-up, and exposed collusion, laxity and inefficiency somewhere down the line. This had not been taken kindly by the 'big-shot's' kinsmen, who dominated other ethnic groups in the Ministry. They said he had disgraced their brother. That was not all. Unassessed opinion, generally heard in certain circles, indicated an imbalance in the allocation of certain strategic posts in the civil service on tribal basis. Martin's kinsmen had a larger proportion and there was pressure from an influential group to offset that imbalance. Martin's removal from office was therefore understandable. It was a victory for some; for others it was a calamity.

Martin's thoughts were again interrupted. This time by a faint knock on the door. He opened it, and there, huddled before him, were his domestic staff – gardener, driver, cook, steward and office messenger (the only relative he had employed in the Ministry). The news of his removal had shocked them. They stood there with their hands behind their backs. They said nothing. They were all in tears. Martin understood. After all, he had been kind to them; he had treated them like human beings. They were not all his kinsmen but he was convinced about their sincerity.

He thanked them for their kind gesture and promised he would see that they remained in their jobs. As they retreated, the gardener ventured. 'Make Master take it like a man.' The rest shook their heads in total agreement; the cook even pronounced the word 'Amen' with an emphasis that brought their hands unconsciously into a clasp across their chests. They then retreated – all of them – tearful with gratitude.

Now that he was alone, Martin decided he would do some telephoning. He would telephone one of his closest friends, a member of the policy and strategic group – the group that laid down government policy, and took far-reaching decisions for the country. This, however, turned out to be a great disappointment. His friend had asked through the steward what he wanted to speak to him about. This was only the beginning of a series of such unexplained behaviour by his closest colleagues. Some found excuses for putting him off.

Others were too busy to speak to him over the telephone on purely official matters. He could no longer understand them.

Some of these very people had flooded his house when he had been appointed to the post. They had brought bottles of champagne with them to celebrate his promotion. They had wished him well. They had come for favours; many still owed him money he had loaned to them. His house had virtually been turned into a guest house. People came from far and near without prior notice and expected to be housed and fed. In spite of this, his removal from office had drawn little or no sympathy. He tried to complain; he even made representations. He was surprised at this general attitude towards him which was characterised by undisguised apathy.

He had heard it said that there was a tendency for the society to stick to successful people and shun them like the plague once their star began to fade. So this was it! His star had faded. He was now nobody. He had been dumped on the scrap heap.

When he thought of all these happenings in retrospect, he agreed he must be fair to himself. After all, he had had his fair share of the huge national cake. There were those who had not even a ghost's chance of doing so. And when later that evening he dropped in at his favourite night-club, to drown his spirits with beer, he found the familiar crowd.

The air was stuffy and acrid with cigarette smoke and many couples were jammed on the small dance floor. The lights had been dimmed intentionally and the usual promiscuous rubbing of backs and buttocks was going on. He took a seat away from the rest of the crowd and took stock of the scene before him.

The faces were familiar – most of them staff of his ministry. It appeared there was some celebration going on. They were celebrating his exit. How unsympathetic! There were bottles of champagne standing on the vacant tables half empty. There was his Personal Secretary, dancing with his Number Two, who was to take his place, her arms round his neck, his arms round her waist, and her head on his shoulder. When the orchestra stopped and the couples returned to their tables, he ventured to the bar, sat on one of the high stools, his back to the crowd and ordered a drink.

While the orchestra was having a brief respite and the celebration had resumed, it appeared an argument was going on, on the merits of good champagne. Martin's successor, the centre of interest, was giving his expert opinion. 'You know what a good champagne does?' he asked with an air of importance. 'I'll tell you. It aids digestion, straightens the muscles, cleanses the blood, washes the liver, tickles the kidneys, warms the bowels, cheers you up, and,' he continued, lowering his voice almost to a whisper, 'gives you a good erection'. The men in the group roared with laughter. The women, too embarrassed, were content with suppressed giggles.

But the celebration ended almost abruptly. The bang of the cork of a champagne bottle, as it hit the ceiling, drew the attention of the group towards the bar. It was only a brief interruption, but enough to provide the subject for another little lecture, still by his successor. This time, on the expertise required to 'kill' a bottle of champagne. A little demonstration then followed. There was only a muffled hiss and the bottle lay open in front of them all – not a drop was spilt. The group cheered loud and long.

Then it happened. It was his Personal Secretary who first spotted him. The word soon went round. One by one, they disappeared. The tables were soon empty. No speeches. No votes of thanks. The party had ended impromptu. The waiters stood aghast – staring at the half a dozen or so half-emptied bottles of champagne, the half-emptied glasses and the smouldering cigarettes in the ashtrays. They looked at each other, shrugged their shoulders in unison and avoided the tables.

Martin's sun had set. *No condition is permanent.* How forcibly struck he was by the words of that popular song! Would his sun rise again? That depended on a few human circumstances, like blood or marital connections, ethnic affinity and sometimes money to pay. How fast, depending on whether your godfather was a 'heavy weight' or just 'paper weight'. Now, where would he start ? Would he have to join the throng of boot-lickers? The trend of his thoughts was broken by a mild stir that was going on around him.

The dramatic exit by the establishment's regular customers, had greatly upset the management. The manager appeared and looked very worried. The place was empty – his lone customer was Martin Ngombe, who was sitting at the bar.

'Monsieur le Secrétaire Général, how nieze to see you. How war you? Very fine? Goot . . .? Very goot?' Martin tried to explain that he was no longer Secretary General, and that he had just been relieved of his post. The manager expressed great surprise, and added: 'Wither you steel there or not, vous êtes toujours le Secrétaire Général.'

And when Martin later left the night-club after the manager had offered him another champagne, his head was in a whirl but under no delusions whatever. He had lost his post and dumped on the scrap heap like the rest.

Two years went by. Martin still remained on the scrap heap. It had not been very easy settling down with his family in the village which they had scarcely visited. The children were his particular worry. They had grown up in the city, in a government villa with adequate modern facilities. They had, for instance, been used to sitting on a toilet-bowl. The change necessitated their squatting on a pit latrine. They could not manage it!

For him, there was no choice. His daily office attire changed from the three-piece suit to a loose shirt and loin-cloth which he expertly bunched around his waist. He got accustomed to drinking the local palm-wine and joined in the general daily routine of village life. He had resigned himself to his fate. He had grown too thick-skinned. Limunga, his wife, was different. She had grown bitter and frustrated with the passing months. She had tried in vain to persuade her husband to get his friends within the corridors of power to make an 'intervention' on his behalf. He had bluntly refused: 'I won't lick dirty feet.' He was firm and, as if to console her, added in Bakwerri, 'Lind i a ja,' meaning 'What must come, will come.'

That was why he had gone in hook-line-and-sinker with the Green Revolution. He had established a yam, plantain and cocoyam farm. This proved a failure. The crop failed. There was no immediate explanation as to why the crop had withered, after the first three months had shown such promise. Not even the local research centre could immediately diagnose the cause. A creeping drought, some said. Others, poor and unscientific methods of farming. There was even the suggestion that the farming seasons ought to be changed.

Thank God, the 'machine' was still paying his salary – paying his salary for doing nothing! How lucky he had been. Others had suffered during the 'machine's' occasional temperamental and erratic moods, when it either refused to pay anything at all, or made arbitrary deductions. He had every reason to be grateful to God for His mercies, he thought. His sun had not set, after all! Despite all his problems, he felt completely at peace with himself. He had never felt like this before!

Two years, three months and five days had passed since Ngombe's exit. Things had not been easy with his successor at the Ministry. It appeared that a power struggle had developed among the staff, resulting in divided loyalties, indiscipline, inefficiency and the divulging of official secrets. All these developments had hampered the smooth and urgent discharge of government business. Grievances, founded and unfounded, were being nursed. Matters had come to a head. The result was a public outcry and the demand for an inquiry into the whole set up. Evidence was accumulated. It was 'relevant', 'frank', 'incisive' and 'damaging'. There were allegations of tribalism, nepotism, favouritism, bribery and corruption all along the line, and the mismanagement of public funds. The report of the inquiry revealed the faces behind the mask, apportioned blame, sometimes scathingly, and made its recommendations.

Government reaction was swift. The axe fell; many heads rolled. But the great surprise was Martin's reinstatement and re-assignment to a much higher post. The news had, as usual, been broadcast over the national radio net-work.

Martin's little village was in festive mood. His clansmen drummed their puffed chests. 'We too have arrived,' they boasted. 'After all, we too are entitled to our fair share of the national cake. Oye . . . Oye . . .' For them it was another victory – they had carved another niche in the hierarchy of the civil service. Messages of congratulation started pouring in from far and wide. They totalled more than one hundred by the end of the week.

Now was the time for lip homage; time to cement strained and thawed relationships; time to strengthen the fraternity. There were personal visits from relations, tribesmen, well-meaning friends; also the hypocrites and the brazen-faced. The cartons of champagne, whisky, brandy, gin and the rest were delivered – after all, he was now in control of one of the strategic ministries.

Ngombe realised the real testing-time was now ahead of him. He was committed to the strict implementation of policies which would help improve the tarnished image of the Ministry. He had to evolve a system that would minimise the disappearance of employment dossiers, dealing with corres-pondence and enquiries expeditiously; hasten claims and payments, and so on, and so forth. 'That's what I'll do. I must do that . . . yes . . . it's a commitment . . .' he was saying, when someone woke him from his reverie.

'You were saying something . . .?' It was his wife. He blinked for a while and then turned to her. 'Yes . . . as I was saying, it's my commitment. You see . . . I've got to change the damned system . . . give it a completely new look. You see my point, don't you?'

Limunga smiled at her husband. 'I know you will, and don't forget that's why they've forked you off the scrap heap.' She was happy. Her husband looked a completely changed man. He looked himself, and more. He looked happier, more determined and more confident.

'Well, that's it. We're going back, aren't we?' Ngombe began, getting up from the chair. 'And I told you so, didn't I?' he continued, laughing. 'Lind i a ja – what must come will come. And, here we are!' He took her hand, pulled her closer in a warm embrace and hugged her, and she cried softly over his shoulder.

So Good to Die

There was a loud screeching of brakes. Then a terrific bang. The little car, hit from the rear, rolled down the slope. There was a violent shock and the deafening noise of crashing and twisting metal as the car finally came to rest at the bottom of the valley, the four wheels up-turned like a turtle forced to lie on its back, waving its limbs helplessly.

Four hours later, Francis Efesoa started regaining consciousness. His head was in a spin. His whole body ached. There was the jabbing pain down his feet and left shoulder. He tried to move, but he realised he had been strapped in splints. He opened his eyes. The lights in the room were strong and bright and he soon realised he was in unfamiliar surroundings. He raised his right hand with some effort to his forehead. Someone took the hand and he could hear a voice saying something like, 'It's alright, please, don't move.'

He opened his eyes again. He could only see her face and the little white skull-cap. A nurse, he thought, as he surveyed the room. There was a chest of drawers on which stood an empty flower vase. Two very large windows on opposite sides with blue curtains. A spare bed on the other side of the room covered with a red blanket and beside him a gleaming silver trolley with an equally gleaming array of instruments in a bowl – syringe, forceps, scissors, etc.

So this was a hospital, he thought. He was trying to say something. The understanding nurse moved closer, her ear almost touching his mouth to listen to what he wanted to say. 'Nurse, I am in great pain,' he whispered hoarsely. The nurse took his hand and assured him he'd be alright. But as the pains grew unbearable, he started to whimper and before he knew, he was crying. The tears coursed down his cheeks on to the pillow and the nurse removed her handkerchief and wiped them. When he opened his eyes again, she too was weeping softly. Ashamed that she had been caught unable to control her emotions, she immediately turned her back to him and hurriedly wiped her tears.

Efesoa had both legs fractured, a dislocation of the left shoulder and a head concussion. 'I am going to die,' he told her again and again. She realised she had to do something to relieve him of the pains. 'I am going to give you some tablets which will help deaden your pains and put you to sleep.' Not long after he had taken the tablets, he started feeling quite relaxed. His eyelids were becoming heavy. They finally drooped and sleep overcame him.

Efesoa had been involved in a serious road accident. His car had been hit from the rear by a 'mammy-waggon' carrying passengers along a straight stretch of road. His little car had been thrown off the road on to the grass verge, then down a steep slope into a valley. He had been brought into hospital with multiple injuries and covered all over with blood. Dr. Slazenger, the hospital surgeon had been called to examine him. He later examined the X-rays carefully and concluded it was a case for a major operation.

The patient started worrying when he knew that they would take him to the theatre. 'What are they going to do with me?' he had inquired of the nurse. 'The doctor wants to set your bones right again, that's all,' she said soothingly, holding his hand and wiping the sweat from his brow. 'I suppose you are going to put me to sleep first, won't you?' he went on. 'Yes, of course,' the nurse replied curtly. 'You think I'll be alright after that? They are not going to amputate any of my broken limbs?' he inquired anxiously. 'Oh . . . no, . . . no,' she assured him with a smile. Then he asked for some cold water to drink. How thirsty he was! He would have preferred a bottle of cold beer. But how unfortunate – they did not serve beer in hospitals.

At 8.30 p.m. prompt, the door of the ward opened and the surgeon appeared. The nurse followed closely behind. He was a young man. Francis guessed he was in his early thirties. His face was narrow, he wore his hair short and sported luxurious side burns, well and neatly groomed. He came round to the bed and patted his patient on the shoulder. 'How are you feeling now?' the doctor asked. 'I have pains in my legs and shoulder, and a splitting headache, Doctor,' he replied wearily, looking straight into the surgeon's eyes. 'Oh, that's normal in a case of this kind, especially on the first day. You will feel better after the operation,' he assured him. Two white-clad male nurses brought a stretcher and the nurse and surgeon helped him on to it.

The theatre room was spacious and devoid of any furniture. The lights were bright and everything glittered. There were two other persons standing around and both assisted in getting Francis on the theatre 'slab.' He could now only see the surgeon's back. He was washing up. When he turned round, he was examining one of the X-rays. He signalled to the nurse, who moved towards the 'slab' and tried to make the patient comfortable. She then took his right arm and laid it on a wooden support with the palm of his hand open. She turned her back and started fiddling with the syringe. So this was it, he thought. They were going to give him an anaesthetic – to make him sleep, so that he would not feel the pain during the process of mending his broken bones.

But they had not checked on his heart-beat! He had heard that people with weak hearts just died in their sleep! Was this going to happen to him? Was he going to die with only the surgeon and nurse around him? There was no time now to say farewell to his old mother. If it happened, she would die of grief! The trend of his thoughts was suddenly broken when the nurse announced that she was going to give an injection. Francis suddenly found himself telling the nurse to hold on. He wanted to say his prayers. The nurse was not a little surprised and held back the syringe.

The surgeon who had been watching patiently, came to the 'slab' to find out what was the matter. 'He wants to say his prayers,' the nurse whispered to the surgeon. Francis closed his eyes and prayed. He asked God to forgive his sins. His old mother was still alive and would die of grief if God allowed him to die. But if he died, God should take him to heaven.

When he opened his eyes again, the operating team was ready. The surgeon came to him and assured him all would be well. The nurse took his arm again and after strapping a piece of elastic around it, took up the syringe. She raised it high above her head against the light and took his arm. Impulsively, his hand grabbed her arm as the needle pricked the skin. The nurse ordered him to relax. He obeyed. There was a slight pain in the arm and that was all.

It all happened very quickly as he lay looking up at the ceiling. His vision was becoming blurred. The figures around him were dancing, as he counted, one . . . two . . . three . . . four . . . five . . . six . . . he soon lost the count. The figures were fading, receding and the hushed conversation which had been going on ceased.

Outside the hospital gates, tension was mounting. Visitors to the scene of the accident had concluded, from what they had seen of the battered car, that Francis had died. Orders had been given by the hospital authorities not to allow any visitors. This helped to confirm some false rumours that a team of doctors were making a desperate effort to save his life. The lone gate-keeper could no longer control the crowd. The doctors held a five-minute conference and decided to issue a statement – a very brief statement.

It was simply that Mr. Efesoa had been involved in a serious accident and was being treated for shock and multiple fractures. He was presently in no grave danger but no visitors would be allowed until further notice. The statement was announced to a near-hysterical mob that had gathered and continued to gather around the hospital, persuading those who had just arrived to return home. Others took the statement for what it was worth – a subtle device to hide the true facts, in order to pacify the mob. They hung around in groups, talking in low tones and moving towards the hospital gates in eager anticipation of some news of the patient, whenever an important-looking hospital employee showed up.

The operation had lasted five hours. The two legs were put in casts. The shoulder was set right and bandaged.

When he woke later, he was back in the ward. He was in pain again! The splitting headache still lingered. A week later the headache was causing some concern to the doctors. It was now being accompanied by a sharp jabbing pain just below the loins. Some days later he started feeling a numbness of the right leg. A further examination revealed that his spine had also been injured. Soon the numbness affected the right arm also, and some weeks later the right side of his body was lifeless, paralysed. The pains in the legs had suddenly disappeared. But that headache! It was impossible to see clearly when it came on. Sometimes he lay unconscious, in a coma, and these lapses had become more frequent as the weeks slipped by. Whenever he regained consciousness, there were a lot of people standing around the bed in helpless abandon, sad and tearful. And sometimes he could read their thoughts: 'He had not died after all. He only fainted.'

During one of those bouts, there had been a lot of movement around him. There was the doctor trying to take his pulse. He recognised his uncle and sister. There too, was his hospital companion – the nurse. The doctor was saying something. He could not hear, but he observed his gesture – a helpless shrug. The group turned their attention to the figure on the bed, grief and compassion written clearly on their faces, their eyes moist with tenderness.

They were all sorry he was going to die. But what would happen to 'Iya', his mother? They would have to put her in chains. That was what they did to her when Mola Njoh died. She said she would kill herself! She had mourned for four years. Would she, too, die of grief?

Of what use was a cripple anyway? He knew he would never walk again. He had seen people hobble around on wooden crutches. Ugly things they were, hurting you under the armpits. You could neither travel fast nor do long distances. You were helpless, a burden, useless – plaguing everybody! No. He was ready to die. He was not afraid of dying. In fact, he was anxious to die. But dying at the age of thirty-five. What a shame. They called that premature. He looked down at his legs, now lifeless and numb. At College he had been the one hundred metres champion. He had captained the College football team. He had even played tennis. He tried to recollect the names of the places he had been to . . . England, America, Israel, Nairobi, Dakar, Lagos . . . he soon lost count. What would happen to his clothes? Who would be wearing them? Would they strip that wreck of a car that had killed him, leave the 'carcass' by the wayside to remind reckless drivers of the dangers on the roads? Now, he was dying, to be locked in a box and put six feet deep underground to avoid his offending stench!

A vague feeling of guilt engulfed him. He had done a few things he was ashamed of. He wished he could say how sorry he was to individuals he had wronged. That bribe he had taken. No. It was not a bribe. He had not demanded it. It had simply been brought to him. They called that a 'dash'. There was the little amulet he carried always in his pocket. He had to carry it. Not that he worshipped it. It was someone else's suggestion. It was to protect him, insulate him, from the clutches of the wicked. He was a big man now, and many people had become envious of his position. And he had succumbed! He realised it was not too late to make amends.

How relieved he felt when Father McCormack called at the hospital on his daily visits. 'How are you feeling now, Francis?' he asked, taking his hand. 'It's my head, Father. That terrible headache. Right here, at the back of my head.' Father McCormack looked at him calmly, 'Oh, you'll be alright. There's no need to worry. . .' he said confidently. He too! Trying to conceal the truth that he was going to die? 'But, it's all wrong, Father, I know I am going to die. Would you listen to my confession?' His tone was agitated. Father McCormack was completely taken aback by his reply. Impulsively, he grasped his hand. 'Come on, Francis, don't talk like that', he cut in soothingly. 'Christ is our hope . . . and . . .' He had not finished before Francis interrupted. 'Father, would you listen to my confession?' He was now pleading.

Resigned, Father McCormack waved to the onlookers. They understood and withdrew. 'Bless me Father, for I have sinned. This is my last confession . . .' and he went on confessing all, everything. He took some time trying to recollect everything. In the end, it had all sounded to him incredibly trivial and not very sinful. 'And here, Father, take this away from me.' He handed the leather amulet to him. They recited the Act of Contrition together, and when they had started saying the Rosary, Efesoa had insisted he would finger the beads himself. The prayer over, Francis received the rite of the anointing of the sick and the Blessed Sacrament. *He had now made Peace with God.* Nothing mattered much anymore.

87

He was ready to die.

He slipped into a shallow pool of sleep. He felt himself soaring up, up and up like a bird on the wing. No. It was like sitting on a swing. It swung upwards, remained suspended for a while and swung downwards – a sensation of rising and falling. When he opened his eyes again, there were more people in the room. He was suffocating, gasping for breath. The faces were growing blurred and appeared to retreat. They put something over his nose. The air rushed into lungs again and he was rising again, up, up, up. He opened his eyes again. Just as he had guessed, it was that ugly contraption – the oxygen equipment – that had revived him.

He had nearly forgotten. He had some savings. How silly of him to forget. He waved to his mother. 'There is my bank book, somewhere in the wardrobe. Get it before someone else does.' His mother said nothing, and he wondered whether she had heard him. 'I have left some money for you, Mama.' He could see she was hurt. Tears welled in her eyes.

My God, why didn't it happen. What grief and agony he was causing to all these people! There were faces he had not seen for a long time. There was his aunt, for instance, who had not been on speaking terms with his mother. What a good thing his dying had done, bringing them together again.

He had almost forgotten his hospital companion. He wanted to say how grateful he was for all the care. What a shame that death was going to cheat her and all these people. He had been thinking of getting married to her since his admission into hospital. He would now have to wait for her in heaven. They would get married there.

Now, what was wrong with him? His thoughts were running riot. No. They were bordering on fantasy. Yes. Absurd but thrilling fabrications. There was such a thing as hallucination. Or was he getting mad? He should have known that no marriages were contracted in heaven!

What time was it now? What day of the week? What date? He could not now remember. It had been just one continuous day. The night did not come again! Not that he cared now – he would soon be going away anyway.

How fortunate that he was not leaving a widow behind.

That unprogressive tribal custom which deliberately starved the widow. She was not allowed to eat until her husband was buried! She was made to sit on the bare floor beside what remained, a lifeless mass of soon festering flesh. You were then called a corpse. They put you out in the open before laying you 'in state'. And if it started raining suddenly, everyone else took shelter and you were left there alone. The curtain was now about to fall, cutting off the living from the dead. Their roads had forked.

His family would be putting out an obituary in the Radio Tit-Bits Programme. His friends would soon hear he had died – 'gone the way of all flesh'. Yes. That was the expression. They would be saying a lot of nice things about him by the grave side. When he was born, where he went to school, his achievements, his exemplary Christian life, and so on, and so forth . . . Then the tears, the flutter of handkerchiefs, the blowing of noses by your dear and loved ones as you were lowered, the patter of loose earth on the coffin like rain on a thatch roof . . . Then silence . . . dead silence . . .

Efesoa would have loved to write his own *In Memoriam*. Something like this:

> *In ever loving memory of our dearly beloved son and brother, who departed this life for eternity . . .*

No. That didn't sound nice . . . too bookish . . . yes . . .

> *Who slept in the Lord*

That was better. And he would add in quotation marks:

> *'It's so good to die.'*

Nothingness closed in once more. He was rising again, taking-off. Then a glorious and triumphal sensation, like the climax at a musical festival, engulfed him. The spotlight trailed him as he walked on the stage. He was the leading star of the performance. An excited and appreciative audience applauded. This was the end of the act. He bowed gracefully before the curtain finally fell. Francis Efesoa had died.

The Raving Masquerade

The seething crowd pressed and jostled on either side of Ogui Road. Everyone wanted to watch the most dreaded Masquerade on parade. Many a time it strode well ahead of the drummers and dancers. Then it would stop suddenly, look above the crowd, turn right, then left and perform a fifty yards dash which raised screams from women and children and sent the crowds stampeding. Further progress was only arrested by an attendant who tugged at the rope secured around the Masquerade's middle.

An approaching whirlwind also added to the fun. There was noisy pushing and shoving as it swept through the crowd stirring the dust and leaves into a moving pillar of brown smoke with hats, caps and headties following in its wake.

Then the Masquerade turned in my direction. 'Click, click,' went the shutter and as I busied myself trying to wind the spool, I heard the crowd yell: 'Bwa Oso! Oso!' I looked up to see what was happening. And there it was – the raving Masquerade. It had run amok. The hideous thing was after me. But what had I done?

I had read about the fate of big game hunters, who combined this sport with the shooting of motion pictures of the denizens of our African jungles and of how many of them had been mauled to death by raving wild game. This is exactly what confronted me. My object was, however, not wild game. It was a Masquerade. I knew it was a man wearing a hideous mask, but I could not stand the sight, and certainly not when it brandished what appeared to me to be a blood-stained cutlass.

I gripped my camera tightly by the strap, fighting against terror – forcing myself to remember the rule that has always guided me – *don't lose your head in an emergency*. But I had never thought of what to do when confronted by a raving Masquerade.

The crowd gave way as I darted frantically across the street and over the open drain in an attempt to escape its fury.

I had just completed a three months 'initiation' course at the Nigerian Broadcasting Corporation Staff Training School in Lagos. That was in 1958. My posting was Enugu as News Reporter. I had been doing a bit of freelance writing – plays, short stories and articles – before I joined the Broadcasting Corporation. The knowledge acquired during this course under the then Head of News, Mr. Norman England, only fired me to still greater heights in freelance writing. I had bought myself a camera to illustrate a series of articles I had been assigned to write for an Overseas Magazine under the title 'Christmas in Odd Places'.

It was Christmas Day in Enugu. You could hear the distant throbbing of drums. There was faint wood smoke in the air, mingled with the flavour of roasting goat meat. You could breath it everywhere!

It was interesting to watch the human flotsam and jetsam reeling along the streets. Their moods varied. There were the drunks who spat and cursed or occasionally broke into hysterical giggles. The happy ones who sang very lustily, cracked jokes, went off into peals of laughter, so infectious that the rest joined. There were others who just walked along as if in a trance, their faces blank and devoid of expression.

The women had finished entertaining their friends and relatives and had now joined in the merry-making. There was the usual tittle-tattle too, most of it idle gossip. Everyone was in Christmas mood.

The children were not out of the show. You could hear the explosion of fireworks and toy-guns. Occasionally, they besieged a passer-by with the cheerful greeting: 'Merry Christmas' or cries of 'Saar, Biko Bwaram Christmas'. On Christmas Day there is everywhere and in everyone a change of heart and so whether you are a stranger or not, it is: 'Saar Bwaram Christmas' or 'Saar, make Me Christmas'.

When I walked down Ogui Road from the Secretariat Quarters that afternoon, I scarcely imagined I was in for an adventure. Christmas 1958 was being celebrated with a zest and flavour unsurpassed by previous Christmases. Not since 1947 when I arrived in Enugu. The only comparison was the West Indian Carnival. You would think it was an organised rally of 'masquerades'. There were small ones. There were big ones. There were multi-coloured masks adorned with multifarious odds and ends. You got the impression that the various communities which made up the population of Enugu were out to out-do one another in this unique Christmas celebration.

There was the 'Ekpo' masquerade and the 'Ntimi' Dance of the Efiks. The 'Ojonu' masquerade and the famous 'Atilogwu' Dance of the Ibos. The 'Ekpete' Dance by the beautiful women of Bonny in the Rivers State. The children were also represented. The 'Ogada' by little girls and 'Sawa' by the boys.

I had been stalking the 'Masquerade' for about a mile. Each time I raised my camera, it either turned its head away or started dancing. This particular Masquerade dance was performed only once a year. This explains why it drew such crowds.

He was a big hulking brute. The headgear was a monstrous, carved wooden mask. The face had a wide gaping mouth displaying teeth filed to points. This gave the Masquerade that looping satanic grin.

Over the body was a costume woven from strands of fibre and raffia. Fastened about its middle was a rope which the attendant tugged from time to time to prevent the Masquerade from going too near the crowd. Occasionally the attendant, who also carried a grass-woven fan, waved it vigorously to prevent the Masquerade from suffocating under the heavy mask.

Then there was a group of about eight sweating young men all stripped to the waist. Accompanying them were six others who played the masquerade dance music. Two of them sounded gongs, another struck a hollowed piece of wood; the third played on the familiar native flute operated by the thumb and forefinger. The two others sat astride drums.

The dance group had called at the house of the landlord who was a prominent personality in the community. He was a middle aged man with a tired, patient humourous face. He must have felt greatly honoured. He grinned from ear to ear as he made a short speech which was greeted by loud cheers. Then followed the ceremonial breaking of kola-nuts and pots of palm-wine were brought for their entertainment.

The leader of the dancing group, a short man with a strong and rather cynical hook-nosed face, stepped forward and with a graceful sweep of the hand, the drummers and flautist started warming up. The flautist began with a monotonous shrill wail, the drummers pounded madly at the drums – their bellies resting on the edge of the drums and their heads thrown back. The drum beats mounted to a frenzied throbbing crescendo as the dancers joined in.

The dance was a sort of gymnastic display but more vigorous and artistic. It consisted of leaps and a thousand-and-one arm, foot, head and body movements with the earth shaking to their rhythm. In a few minutes, the dancers were glistening and dripping with sweat. What an entertaining display it was!

I had forgotten all about the Masquerade, when it suddenly appeared, as if from nowhere. The crowd retreated as it walked round the dancers, brandishing the cutlass and the attendant tugging desperately at the rope.

So far, there had been no incidents. An appeal to the public had been made by the Urban District Council against the hooliganism and recklessness which had so often been associated with Christmas festivities in the past. The Broadcasting Corporation carried a statement by the Chairman, warning that troublemakers would be dealt with ruthlessly by the forces of law and order. It was a real show of strength. The police were on beat duty – two on a single beat – equipped with safety helmets, whicker-shields and batons. A police patrol car swooped past now and again, its siren wailing in its wake. There was also a Black Maria which was parked nearby to whisk drunks and troublemakers off to their temporary detention – an atmosphere of gaiety, revelry and of a town under siege.

I raised my camera at the ready as the Masquerade turned in my direction and just as I pulled the trigger, someone brushed past me, ruining all my efforts of the past thirty minutes. I was furious, shouted angrily at him, but he was so absorbed in the scene before him that he took no notice of my outburst. All I had to do was to wait.

Then he turned round again facing me. 'Click . . . click' and the shutter closed. I had got him! I turned round contentedly and began to wind the spool, but decided to take another shot, just in case. I got the second shot; then it happened. All of a sudden, I heard the crowd yell. 'Bwa Oso . . . Oso . . .'. I was completely taken off my guard, for the brute was almost on me when I turned round. Like the timely movement of the matador confronted by an enraged bull, I swerved deftly to the right. He came tearing down at me in all fury, missed me by inches and crashed into a nearby tree stump. He gathered himself up almost immediately and broke-free as the attendant seemed to have lost grip of the rope which was securely fastened around his middle. Then the race began.

I was not wearing a track-suit or anything near it. You can imagine what it was like, running in a suit. I had no time to take off my jacket. *Don't lose your head in an emergency* – that was the rule that had always guided me. Now, it struck me forcefully. Now, *Ndeley Mokoso*, don't panic, my inner voice kept telling me. I tried the one hundred yards dash gripping my camera tightly by the strap, my aim being to escape its fury by putting as much distance between us as possible.

The crowd gave way as I darted frantically along the street. The Masquerade followed. I could hear the jingle of its ankle-bells behind me. I looked back now and again to check on my progress. He was still tearing down in my direction, and no one could stop him; he had gone berserk with rage. The crowd was now cheering.

But where were the police! Why had they not arrived! What if I got mauled by this thing before they arrived! It would certainly be too late then.

Then my breathing started coming on in short gasps. I realised I was tiring and my vision was becoming blurred. I looked back; it appeared that the Masquerade was slowing down too. Then the distant wail of the police-car siren came to me; too far it appeared then. The crowds ran helter-skelter as the police pulled up.

I do not recollect what happened after that. It appeared that I had blacked-out while on my last lap, just before the police arrived, still holding on to my camera. They said I had suffered from shock and exhaustion.

Beside me, in hospital, was the Masquerader. The story was that he too had got out of breath under the heavy mask. They had first of all laid him down on the grass verge and virtually torn the mask off his face. He looked over at me, a puzzled look that started giving me an idea. I stared at him taking in the details. I thought his face was quite familiar. I was sure I had seen that face before. Certainly; there was no mistake about that! I recognised him. He was the wayside bicycle repairer who did the monthly servicing of my Raleigh bicycle. He was Clement Ibeziako, alias Doctor of Bicycle, of Ogui-Ofemili.

We just stared at each other, I saying nothing, he saying nothing. Then I ventured. 'Ibe, how did it happen?' 'M-m-mas-s-ster,' he stammered. 'So dis palaver is between us two, you and myself? Oh . . . sorry . . . sorry . . . God forbid it . . .' he continued, taking the praying posture of Catholics when saying the Lord's Prayer at Mass. He must have read my thoughts, for he added apologetically, 'Master, biko, I beg no vex . . . biko . . . biko . . .' I accepted his apology with a nod and a smile.

The Mistake

'I'm leaving your house this minute. I shan't stay here any longer. You bully of a husband.' Ngozi's brittle voice crackled with scorn. Her eyes flashed angrily as the neighbours freed her from Nwankwo's grip. The furniture in their little room lay about in complete confusion. On her left cheek Nwankwo's five finger impressions showed clearly. She sobbed quietly as she searched for her missing ear-ring that had dropped during the scuffle.

Nwankwo, her husband, stood with his back to the door, barring her exit. His massive chest heaved rapidly. Bright red blood sparked from the index finger of his right hand.

'See what you've done . . . nearly bitten off my finger,' he scowled, his eyes filled with rage. You must understand that I wear the trousers in this house. My instructions must be carried out. You don't think I paid for your education – and £120 as dowry to your father – to be disobeyed?'

'That's the reason for beating me, is it?'

'If you take it that way . . . yes,' he mocked. She brushed past him into the adjoining room and in a moment there came the clatter of trunk boxes. Ngozi was packing.

The trouble had started with a little row that evening. Nwankwo had suddenly remembered that they had arranged a billiards match with his club mates that evening.

'Ngozi,' he called. 'Is my dinner ready? I've just remembered we'd arranged a billiards match at the club tonight. I'm already getting late.' His wife did not reply. Nwankwo felt so annoyed.

'You heard what I said. I want my dinner,' he added firmly.

'You stay where you are. You are doing no clubbing tonight. You are always around there with that gang like a lot of hooligans!' Ngozi's voice rang out with contempt.

'Oh, shut up,' he interrupted. 'I am all day at the office; aren't I to have some fun?'

'Fun my foot,' she challenged. 'I telephoned the club the other night. It was you who answered the telephone – I recognised your voice. You remember? When I said I wanted to speak to Mr. Nwankwo, you hung-up. Later I was told by someone else that you were not in the club. I later got wind that you were seeing that little bitch with the big "bottom". Whom do you think you are fooling? A little school girl? You should be ashamed of yourself.' Nwankwo did not say a word. He walked to the door and tried to open it. It was securely locked. Furious, he shook it. 'Ngozi,' he flared up. 'What do you think you are doing? Come on, open the door or I'll break it down.'

'Go on, break the door down,' she mocked. Nwankwo surveyed his wife with astonishing mildness. He could see the devil in her eyes. He turned to the door again and shook it violently. 'Let me have the keys, or I'll teach you a good lesson,' he warned, pointing his finger at her.

'Go on,' she repeated, with a sneer on her face. 'What do you think I am? Your kitchen maid? I'll have no more of this – I've had enough.'

'But I must go to the club. We have a match starting soon. Can't you see? We've got everything laid on.'

'Go on, break down the door,' his wife continued to tease him. Nwankwo was staggered by his wife's firmness. This was a humiliation. She had the nerve to challenge him, to confront him! Where the hell did she get this idea! He would teach her a lesson she would not forget. He made up his mind.

He entered the bedroom. When he came out, he was holding his brown leather belt. He rushed at her. She had no time to escape. He swung the belt menacingly and hit her hard on the shoulder. He hit her a second time. She gave a loud scream and tried to hold the belt. Then he slapped her full across the face three times. She retreated into the kitchen trying to find a way to escape her husband's fury. He pursued her as she retreated covering her face with her hands and crying, 'Wuna cam . . . o . . . he don kill me.' She was desperate and tried to fight back, clinging onto him like a limpet, biting and scratching until the neighbours came in to separate them.

Ngozi seemed to have made up her mind to go. Attempts

97

by well-meaning neighbours to settle their dispute proved abortive. Nwankwo made no attempt to stop her, in fact he had welcomed his wife's decision to leave him with some relief. But one thing worried him. The dowry. How was he going to get it back? He had not only paid a high bride price. He had been responsible for her training. She was a trained teacher.

They had both lived together happily until she started observing a change in her husband's behaviour towards her. He had grown sullen and irritable. He was no longer the kind and devoted husband she had known and adored. He was now a bully making her so unhappy and miserable.

Ngozi had tried on several occasions to find out what was wrong but he had dismissed any suggestions about the reasons for his attitude towards her. She had ventured again one evening with the suggestion that he should consult a doctor. 'You will breakdown if you go on like this,' she had warned, her voice soft and troubled.

That Ngozi was deeply concerned about her husband's behaviour, there was no doubt and her fears grew as the weeks slipped by; he had shown no marked improvement.

The trouble started soon after the publication of the Bride Price Commission's Report on 30th October, 1954. The Commission, headed by a Lawyer, was set-up by the then Eastern Region (Nigeria) Executive Council. The terms of reference were 'to investigate the social effects of the payment of bride price in the Eastern Region and to make any recommendations to the Executive Council it might think fit with a view to the removal of any anomaly or hardship.' The Committee submitted its report – a fifty-seven page document – after touring the various divisions of the Region and receiving both oral and written evidence from individuals and tribal organisations. The Commission had in the main recommended the reduction of the bride price. Had he not been impatient, Nwankwo thought, he could have married Ngozi for £90 less. He felt he had been cheated, and so during the following weeks he became indifferent. He just sat and sulked. He started to complain about the way his wife was preparing his meals. Today there was too much pepper in the soup. The next day it was that the yam-foofoo was not well pounded and on many occasions he had refused to eat the food she had cooked.

Nwankwo's campaign did not end there. He had sent a request card to the local Broadcasting Service for the 'Ugly Woman Calypso' to be played for his wife on the occasion of her birthday in the programme 'From me to You'.

Ngozi was busy doing her housework when she heard the announcer's voice: 'It's hello now to Mrs. Ngozi Nwankwo of 84 Ogui Road, Asata, Enugu, who celebrates her birthday today. I hope she is listening. Your husband has asked us to play the "Ugly Woman Calypso" on this occasion. Congratulations and many happy returns.'

In a fit of uncontrollable temper, she had grabbed the nearest object that came to hand. There was a terrific crash and bits of glass lay all over the room. She had flung the flower vase at what remained of the radio-set when Nwankwo appeard.

'Good heavens, what's this?' He could not believe his eyes. 'Smashed my wireless!' his voice choked.

'What did you mean by that "Ug y Woman Calypso" thing you had played for me?' She had grown hysterical and had flung herself onto him. They had fought until the neighbours intervened. They had tried to make it up but it was a short-lived truce. The club incident was the last straw. Ngozi had decided to return to her parents. And she did so.

Nwankwo's campaign ended with Ngozi's departure. He congratulated himself on his victory. Now that she was gone, he was a free man. What's more, there was £120 dowry money to his credit.

He had discussed the situation with his best friend, he himself a married man. This man had expressed great disappointment at what he called a 'reckless pursuit' and had some adverse comments to make on the events leading up to Ngozi's departure.

'What's this disgraceful affair with your wife? Can't you settle it?' he had enquired.

'I don't know what's disgraceful about your wife deciding to leave you. If you've read the Bride Price Commission's

Report which has, in effect reduced Bride Price to £30, you realise I can now marry and still have £90 to my credit,' Nwankwo tried to explain. And when the discussion broke later, Nwankwo could still not be persuaded to reverse his decision. He had been cheated, and whatever his friend thought about the matter, he would pursue the only course now open to him.

For the first few weeks, Nwankwo did not even as much as think of his wife – he was having a good time. But after a few months things took a different turn. The house boy had suddenly decided to go away and Nwankwo soon found that he had to do the cooking himself. He had spent more money during the period than he had at any other time, mostly on drinks. His married colleagues said he was irresponsible and boycotted his company. Before long Nwankwo realised the important part Ngozi had played as his wife. But he was the 'lord and master'. He had paid £120 as dowry. He was not going to ask her to return – his friends would laugh at him. It was clear that Nwankwo had looked at his wife only in terms of money and now he realised he had made a mistake but was not honest enough to admit it.

When Ngozi did turn up at the house six months later, it was not because she wanted to reconcile with her husband. It was to take away her belongings which she had left behind.

'I also forgot to take my wedding ring which you took away from me before I left. We will also have to decide on who should keep that wedding picture,' she said, pointing at the picture which still hung on the wall. 'And if you are going to keep it, you should remove it from its position there.'

'You realise you are still my wife. Don't you?' Nwankwo said, squinting searchingly into his wife's face.

'Confound you,' Ngozi shouted defiantly. She seized the bottle of ink on the table and hurled it at the picture. Down it came with a crash. Nwankwo was too dazed for words. He just stood there looking, whilst she searched the drawers for her wedding ring. And in spite of intervention by the neighbours, Ngozi insisted on returning to her parents. And she did.

The weeks slipped by. Everyday brought its new problems – problems which did not exist when Ngozi was around. His had been a reckless pursuit. Dowry or no dowry, Ngozi now meant so much to him. He needed her now more than ever before.

He took some note-paper, and this time it was another request. It was that the record 'I Wonder Who's Kissing Her Now' be played for his wife.

Ngozi was busy knitting when the announcer's voice came over with another request from her husband. After listening, she came to one conclusion – Nwankwo was growing jealous – and she wondered what he was up to. She had also seen a return of that kindness she had always known. She decided to return to her home.

Later that evening, she knocked on the door. She waited patiently, leaning against the door-post. Two minutes went by; the door opened. A voice said, 'Who is it?' Nwankwo looked with surprise into the smiling face of his wife.

'What did you mean by that "I Wonder Who's Kissing Her Now" thing you had played for me?' she asked, laughing.

'I'm really sorry about that, Honey, but I was getting rather desperate. I knew you would come.'

'And what about the dowry. You still insist on the refund to you of £90, don't you?' she teased him.

'Come, come, I must have completely misunderstood the Bride Price Commission's Report,' he added peevishly as he helped to carry Ngozi's luggage into the house.

Man Pass Man

The referee blew his whistle and ran across the field to find out what the rumpus was all about. The captain of the visiting team was protesting. 'This is the man. This is their juju-man. See what he is carrying in his pockets.' He produced some odd bits of human hair, a length of black sewing thread, a small padlock and some black smelly powder.

John Hilton was furious. 'Look here, you cannot hold up play with this ridiculous story. It's the limit! I'll have no more of this superstitious nonsense about juju in football. Any more interruptions, I'll have no alternative but send you out. You understand that, don't you?' He was firm. He had had enough of these juju-stories during his two years' refereeing in the territory. He took out his notebook and made an entry. But the captain of the opposing team continued his protest. He was joined by the rest who converged on the referee, accusing him of bias and prejudice. He was reminded that he was not refereeing in Wembley Stadium. He was in Africa. 'In Africa you do not dismiss these matters with such contempt. They are part of the life, beliefs and customs of our peoples',' they told him. 'I shall brook no more of this nonsense, customs or no customs. Let that be very clear,' he added, raising a warning finger. That did it. The referee then conferred with the two linesmen, checked his watch and allowed the match to continue.

This incident was triggered by a man who stood by the corner flag. He was tall and thin. He wore a brown felt hat and dark sun-glasses. He removed a white handkerchief from his pocket and wiped his face. Five football fans of the opposing team knew it was the signal – the green light that urged them into action. They ran down the touchline, seized the innocent looking spectator in the flowing robes and beat him unconscious. Two players from the home team left their positions in the field of play to rescue the victim on the touchline. Before the referee realised what was happening, three more players had rushed to the scene and joined in the scuffle.

The occasion was the finals of the Commissioner's Cup Competition. The Woodrow Memorial Stadium was packed full with thousands of football fans from all over the territory. Two top teams had emerged through the semi-finals – the Mountain Wanderers and the Coasters.

The Coasters, a much more formidable and disciplined team, had a good record behind them. The team had been at the top of the League Table for three successive seasons – the never-to-be beaten champions. Their rivals, a newly formed team had only just emerged into the football limelight. There had been many surprises during the season. The Coasters had eliminated the Sputniks, the previous season's semi-finalists, and as the buses and lorries carrying chanting football fans parked outside the stadium gates, it was clear that they were determined to keep the cup for another season.

A few incidents took place before the match actually started. The Wanderers had arrived at the stadium gates led by a man brandishing an ivory-tipped walking stick. He suddenly ordered the players to move back, blocking their entrance. 'Not this way,' he warned briefly. He made a few passes with his stick and pointed to the stadium wall. 'Now, up here, and be quick about it.' Nobody argued or questioned the order. The eleven players and four reserves scrambled over the wall and dropped into the stadium.

A few days earlier, the club's executive had voted the sum of one hundred thousand francs, under miscellaneous expenses, for the transport and upkeep of their juju-man. He was to make it possible for them to win the much coveted cup. They had sent 'spies' to watch the opposing team during their training sessions in order to enable them to plan a strategy for the finals. The team manager and coach had hired a taxi for the two hundred mile journey to Oba to bring the man whose assignment was to avert the disaster which they believed awaited them. They had witnessed the weird process of consulting the oracle – a little object the size of a land-crab studded with cowries. It chirped like a young chick – a language which only one man understood.

The consultation was brief. They were told they would win

103

by two goals if they took a certain line of action. They were to avoid going through the stadium gates and were to insist on using the football provided by the Football Federation.

When the team manager arrived with the man who was to change the tide for the Wanderers, it was imperative that everything possible should be done to stifle the behind-the-scene moves of the opposing team. During the final training sessions the players had been given amulets, which were to be worn under their jerseys, and bits of sewn leather parchments, which they slipped into their boots to prevent sprains and cramps. The goalkeeper had a special meal prepared for him. It consisted of pepper-soup containing the liver of the long-tailed monkey and ripe plantains. To combat the multiplicity of footballs within the 'eighteen', he was given nine office pins which were to be driven into the ground along the goal line. He had sworn that during one of the encounters, three footballs had appeard simultaneously before him as he stood between the goal posts. He had dived for the wrong one and the 'real' ball had found its way into the net.

There was the case of the centre forward of the Sputniks, the best in the territory. He had collapsed during the first encounter with the Coasters who had earlier threatened that they would 'pocket' him. Both teams, therefore, had to invoke counter measures by using 'Kanda-Stick'.

And so, a day before the match, the 'action group' of five members of the home team accompanied by their own witch doctor, entered the stadium at midnight to bury the black sheep. The oracle had ordained the sacrifice of a black sheep. Sentries had been posted around the stadium to prevent any intruders. A hole was dug quickly with picks and shovels. The black sheep was gagged to prevent it from bleating. They produced a cutlass, severed the neck, removed the entrails and threw the still shuddering carcass into the hole, stamped on it with their feet, threw some loose sand over the area and withdrew.

Thousands of football fans from all over the territory, roared their heads off as the teams in their colours ran down onto the pitch. The players then lined up ready to be introduced to the Commissioner.

The Wanderers in their traditional green and white striped jerseys over red shorts; the Coasters in white shirts and shorts. The Commissioner accompanied by the Provincial Chairman of the Football Federation and the Presidents of the two clubs walked down from the VIP stand onto the pitch. They were met by the referee and the two linesmen. The referee introduced his colleagues and turned to the two teams which had lined up facing each other. The captains stepped out in turn, shook hands with the Commissioner and walked by his side, as he, in turn shook hands with the players.

The introductions over, the players took up their positions ready for the kick-off. The Commissioner, an ageing British Colonial Administrator, walked into the centre circle, waited for the referee's whistle and just toed-up the ball. The ball rolled lazily over the touch-line. The crowd cheered as the Commissioner walked back to the grandstand, flanked on either side by the officials.

Then the match started. For the first fifteen minutes the Wanderers were under very great pressure – things were going wrong. Their brilliant forward and powerful striker, Mokoko alias 'Pele', was brought down several times by their opponents' hatchet-man, Ebele alias 'Ziko'. The referee warned Ebele following another dangerous charge on an opponent. He had awarded a free kick from a point just off the centre circle. The ball dropped within the penalty box. Heads went up for it. One head hit it hard and the ball sailed over the bar. The following ten minutes saw a sudden build-up by the Wanderers in their attack which gave their opponents no breathing space. Jean gathered a pass from Sunday. Mokoko raced into a position which left the opposing defence wide open. Left outside Ndumbe gathered the ball and flew on down the touchline. Timing it beautifully, he put in a timely centre. Striker Mokoko moved fast and drove the ball hard and low into the net. This curtain-raiser was followed by a brilliant round of good passing which ended in the ball flying over the crossbar. The field exploded. The crowd cheered hysterically. It was great stuff to watch!

Towards the end of the first half, however, spectators witnessed what became known in the territory's football history as the 'Odd Case'. Odd in the sense that there was so much mystery shrouding the events. Five young stalwarts – all supporters of the visiting team, the Coasters – had a specific assignment. It was to watch over the man in the felt hat who was to give them the lead. He in turn stalked the man in the flowing white robes, who grew restless as he watched the scene before him. The Wanderers were now leading by two goals. The man in the white robes was not alone. It appeared he, too, had his own protection men – two burly fellows who always walked behind him. The ball had been kicked deep into the Coasters' half. The right hand of the man in the white robes went down instinctively into the folds of his clothes, and came out with his fist clenched. He flung whatever he was holding on the ground before him, put his right foot on it, and pressed hard. A few minutes later, the Wanderers' inside right hoodwinked the defence and passed to the centre-forward who had a clear run in on goal. The goal-keeper had no chance with his cracker of a finishing shot. The Wanderers' supporters cheered loud and long, giving their team a five-minute standing ovation.

This was the time. The man in the felt-hat took out his handkerchief and wiped his face. It was the signal. They converged on the man in the white robes. They took him completely unawares. They lifted him off his feet, knocked him on the ground, searched him and took whatever he had in his pockets money and all. Three minutes did the job – the victim was a writhing shuddering heap battered beyond recognition. The two strongmen who had come to his rescue met the same fate.

John Hilton was not aware of the commotion which was now going on until three players had left the field of play and joined in the free-for-all fight that was going on. He stopped the game and ran down the touchline. It was the old story. A man had been influencing the trend of the Cup Final with juju. 'Nonsense,' he said simply, summoned the three offending players and gave them a brief telling-off and a stern warning. The match continued.

Then something happened. The goalkeeper of the Coasters, standing between the posts had an eerie feeling. He walked to both ends of the uprights and inspected the corners. There was nothing. He made two brilliant saves – one, a powerful header from a corner kick, the other a shot from striker Mokoko. As he dropped after saving the shot, his feet sank into the sand. He looked down at his boots. Beneath the sand was fresh loose earth. He suspected something and continued poking at the earth with his right boot. What he saw frightened him – the hind-legs of some animal. He took courage and pulled at the legs. Up came the already decomposing carcass of a black sheep. The discovery caused some sensation. Press photographers invaded the pitch. Spectators converged around the area as news of the black sheep went round.

The match was again held up to allow the stadium officials to arrange the removal of the carcass and the filling up of the holed goal area. When play resumed, it soon became clear that the tide was turning in favour of the Coasters. Spectators witnessed what the press described as 'an onslaught'. The Wanderers seemed no match for the Coasters. They now lacked the confidence, coordination and combination they had exhibited during the earlier half. Too many things went wrong and all at the same time. The Coasters had equalised the score.

Then the Wanderers' goalkeeper had one of those brain-waves. He ran up to the referee just before kick-off to protest against the continued use of the football. He swore he had seen three footballs each time Manga hit the ball. The referee ordered him back to his poet. Thereupon the goalkeeper picked up the ball deflated it with a pin and kicked it off the pitch. As the forwards of the opposing team converged on him, he ran back to the goal. John Hilton blew his whistle and summoned him. He walked back, half running, and stood at attention a few paces from John Hilton. A brief dialogue ensued and the referee showed him the yellow card. The goalkeeper was mollified and immediately went down on his knees appealing to him and trying to justify his action. The referee promptly waved him off and the match continued. Two more goals were scored by the Coasters who maintained their title as the 'never-to-be-beaten-champions'.

It was an hour after the end of the Cup Final that the man in the white flowing robes regained consciousness. He had been taken to hospital soon after he had been attacked. He gave a searching glance and seemed to have assessed the situation. 'The match,' he ventured. 'We won the Cup?' 'We lost the match,' one of the fans tried to explain. 'They unearthed the black sheep, and that sealed our doom.' The man on the bed did not reply. He was sobbing quietly, the tears coursing down his face. The other wiped the tears and tried to console him. 'Come on . . . never mind. We shall live to fight another day. There were too many loose ends in our 'Kanda-Stick' arrangements. It was a matter of Man Pass Man.'